"Who told you about my marriage?"

He hesitated, then said, "The real question should be why didn't you tell me about your marriage? Or about living in France. And writing books. And...and...and everything else. Jeez, Marcy, I flat out asked what you'd been up to for the last fifteen years. Why didn't you tell me any of that stuff?"

She'd actually asked herself that very question after she and Max parted ways the afternoon before. Everyone in Endicott must know what she'd been doing since college. Her name and face had been plastered in every rag in the grocery store checkout lines, and on every splashy celebrity website on the internet. Gossip was the national pastime of her hometown. She'd been amazed yesterday when Max had clearly not known any of it.

Maybe that was why she hadn't filled him in. Because for those few moments with him, she hadn't been Marcella Robillard, disgraced socialite and literary deadbeat who'd written bestselling novels, traveled all over the world and dated some of the most desirable men on the planet before going down in flames. She'd just been Marcy Hanlon from Endicott.

Dear Reader,

I love gardening. Unfortunately, I'm terrible at it and far more likely to kill anything I put into the ground than grow it. So I was delighted when landscaper Max Travers walked into my brain and said, "Hey, I hear you like lobelias..." (They were my grandmother's favorite flower.)

Even better is having his high school crush, Marcy Hanlon, come back to their small town, since I've been married to my high school crush for more than thirty-five years. Best of all, though, she was kind of crushing on him back then, too.

But although love will find a way, sometimes it takes a few detours. There will be secrets and wishes and mix-ups along the way, not to mention a bit of uncertainty. But wish-granting Comet Bob will save the day, as always. He just might want to have a little fun of his own first.

Happy reading!

Elizabeth

Secret under
the Stars

———

ELIZABETH BEVARLY

SPECIAL
EDITION™

Recycling programs
for this product may
not exist in your area.

ISBN-13: 978-1-335-72429-8

Secret under the Stars

Harlequin Enterprises ULC
22 Adelaide St. West, 41st Floor
Toronto, Ontario M5H 4E3, Canada
www.Harlequin.com

Printed in U.S.A.

Elizabeth Bevarly is the award-winning *New York Times* bestselling author of more than seventy books, novellas and screenplays. Although she has called places like San Juan, Puerto Rico, and Haddonfield, New Jersey, home, she's now happily settled back in her native Kentucky with her husband and son. When she's not writing, she's binge-watching documentaries on Netflix, spending too much time on Reddit or making soup out of whatever she finds in the freezer. Visit her at elizabethbevarly.com for news about current and upcoming projects; book, music and film recommendations; recipes; and lots of other fun stuff.

Books by Elizabeth Bevarly

Harlequin Special Edition

Lucky Stars

Be Careful What You Wish For
Her Good-Luck Charm

Harlequin Desire

Taming the Prince
Taming the Beastly M.D.
Married to His Business
The Billionaire Gets His Way
My Fair Billionaire
Caught in the Billionaire's Embrace

Visit the Author Profile page
at Harlequin.com for more titles.

For David.

Here's to high school crushes.

Thanks for forty-four years of wonderfulness. :)

Prologue

"Not again."

"Dude. How many times has it happened?"

"This week? At least ten."

"Nah. It's been ten times this weekend alone."

"Good point. And every time it happens, he looks like he's gonna hurl."

Fifteen-year-old Max Travers barely heard his best friends' exchange. He was too caught up getting lost in the vision on the other side of the pool. Marcy Hanlon. The most beautiful, most charming, most graceful, most excellent… He stifled a sigh. The smartest, kindest, greatest, loveliest… He stifled a second sigh. The most…awesomest human being on the planet. In a hot-pink bikini. Slathering suntan lotion on her ivory shoulders while she chatted with her two best friends at the Endicott Country Club on a bright September afternoon.

Brilliant. She was absolutely brilliant. Radiant, even. Luminous. Max had read that word in a book for English class last week, and after looking it up, all he could think was that it described Marcy perfectly. 'Cause she for sure brought light into every second he was around her, and everything in his life was drab and dull when she wasn't there.

Which was usually. Other than a few scattered times at the pool during the season, he rarely saw her anywhere but school—and there, they only had two classes together this term—and every Saturday, when he went to her folks' house to take care of their garden while his boss, Mr. Bartok, tended the rest of their perfectly manicured estate. And those Saturdays would be coming to an end in a few weeks. Yeah, he could squeeze in an extra month or so freelancing for the Hanlons, but that would be it. Mr. Hanlon hated Max's guts—because, among other things, he probably knew Max had a thing for his daughter—but the old man was smart enough to realize that no one in Indiana could keep his dahlias going longer than Max

Travers could, and no one could get them to bloom earlier in this zone. Once the dahlias were done, though, Max could kiss goodbye any chance of seeing Marcy outside of Biology or Algebra II.

"You should go talk to her," his friend Chance said from his left side. "Ask her what she's doing later."

"Yeah," his other friend, Felix, agreed from his right. "She's with Claire and Amanda. Maybe we can get all three of them to meet us at Deb's Diner for burgers."

Oh, sure. He might as well try to talk to the Queen of Sheba—or Makeda, as his Ethiopian mother had called her in the stories she used to tell Max at bedtime when he was a kid. The Hanlons probably had as much wealth as Makeda and King Solomon combined. No way would they let Max near their daughter. As it was, her three older brothers had been staring daggers at him and Chance and Felix ever since they entered the pool area, thanks to the three of them being working-class scum. The only reason the friends were even allowed at the pool was because it was a perk of their summer jobs—Max worked as a greenkeeper for the club, Felix bused tables in the restaurant and Chance was a lifeguard. But the Hanlon brothers' contempt for Max specifically—and Mr. and Mrs.

Hanlon's contempt, for that matter—went deeper than the economic divide, he knew. There was just way too much melanin on his mother's side of the family.

"I'm not gonna go talk to her," he told his friends, never taking his eyes off Marcy. "Holy crow, that's just an invitation to get pounded by Remy and Percy and Mads."

"Pshaw," Chance huffed theatrically. "Remington and Percival and Maddenford Hanlon wouldn't last two minutes with the likes of us."

"Yeah," Felix agreed. "And who the hell gives their kids names like that? Seriously. That's just an invitation for them to get pounded by their class-mates."

Hah, Max thought. Felix wished. Marcy's broth-ers had all lettered in football and wrestling. He and his two friends would be little more than oily spots in the grass when the Hanlons got through with them.

"At least Marcy's got a name that doesn't take all day to write out," Chance said.

"At least Marcy doesn't think she's better than everyone else in town," Felix added. "Though how she turned out that way, coming from a family like hers, I'll never know."

It was definitely one of Endicott, Indiana's greatest mysteries, Max had to admit. Her father, Lionel Remington Hanlon IV, was, no question, the richest guy in Endicott. He was almost certainly the richest guy in southern Indiana. Hell, he was probably one of the richest—maybe even *the* richest—guy in the whole state. The Hanlons lived in a huge house atop a huge hill just outside of Endicott, one that had been built when the town was just a wayside port on the Ohio. It was surrounded by ten acres, all of it—save the garden—rolling green knobs that overlooked the river. They had a tennis court, an in-ground pool and a stable with three horses. Max had never been allowed to enter the house, but he'd heard there was a bowling alley and movie theater in the basement, along with a huge wine cellar.

And, of course, there was the garden, a half acre that Max both loved and hated tending. Loved because Mr. Hanlon insisted on having some of the most exotic, expensive plants he could find, many of which weren't even suited to Indiana's capricious climate. Hated for the same reason. Every year, Max planted and cared for them as long as the weather would allow, then had to watch them shrivel and die when fall set in, never to return. Then he'd have to pull out their formerly glorious carcasses and turn them into mulch for next year's assortment. It was a crime the way that guy just discarded some of the most beautiful, most perfect things in the world because he didn't have the time or concern for them. He only wanted them as showpieces to flaunt his wealth.

Max looked at Marcy again. She was chatting happily with her friends, not sparing so much as a glance for Max. He didn't take it personally. She wasn't sparing a glance for any other guy, either. Even though there wasn't a guy in Endicott who wouldn't walk over hot coals for her. Felix was right—she was nothing like the rest of her family. They'd sat next to each other in Natural Science for a whole term last year, and they'd been partnered for a week to do a research paper on *The Scarlet Letter* in English. Max had thought the story was pretty tedious and the characters kind of annoying, but Marcy had loved it. Thanks to her enthusiasm, they'd gotten an A on it. And thanks to her being so kind and so smart and so beautiful and so excellent and so perfect, Max had fallen hopelessly in—

"Well, if we're not going to the diner later," Felix said, jarring him back to the present, "then let's hit the club restaurant. They still have some Bob cookies leftover."

Max smiled at the mention of Comet Bob, Endicott, Indiana's sole claim to fame. The comet had been returning to the planet every fifteen years for centuries, always making his closest pass in the skies above their small town. No one knew why. At this point, no one cared why. But the residents of Endicott had come to claim Bob as their own.

Legend had it that anyone born in a year the comet visited—which Max and Chance and Felix had been—could make a wish the next time Bob came around, and then see that wish granted on his third visit, when the wisher was thirty. Max hadn't been immune to the whimsy surrounding the legend of the wishes. In fact, he'd embraced it. All three of them had. A few nights ago, when Bob was directly overhead, he and his friends had sent wishes skyward. Chance had wished for a million dollars. Felix had wished for something interesting to happen in their sleepy little town. But Max…

Max had wished for the most noble thing in the world. True love. He'd wished Marcy Hanlon would see him as something other than the guy who took care of her family's lawn.

"So who wants a cookie?" Felix asked. "They're not giving them to club members, since they're not so fresh anymore, but we wretched refuse can help ourselves. Who's up for a kitchen raid?"

He and Chance were off like a shot, but Max couldn't quite bring himself to leave. Because Marcy had glanced over long enough to catch Max looking at her, and now she was looking back. Then she lifted a hand to offer him a quick wave. And then—*then*—Marcy smiled at him. The most perfect smile Max had ever seen.

But then her brother Remy called her name, and her other brothers came to join her. The looks they gave Max were nothing short of menacing. He didn't care. In fifteen years, none of it would matter. Because in fifteen years, Marcy Hanlon would be out from under her family's thumb, and Bob would be granting his wish.

And Max would be right here in Endicott, waiting for it to happen.

Chapter One

He had been hoping she'd come back to town for the festival this year. He'd been begging Bob—even before the comet appeared on the horizon a couple of weeks ago—to bring her back to Endicott and fulfill the wish he made when he was fifteen. He'd been bolstering himself for weeks, maybe months, so that he wouldn't revert to the tongue-tied, starry-eyed kid he'd been every time he tried to talk to her when they were in high school. He had given himself a dozen pep talks about what a good guy he'd grown up to be, had reminded himself she was an adult woman who was no longer ruled by her family's edicts. He had told himself a million times that the social and economic divide between the two of them when they were kids was meaningless now that they were adults. And he had assured himself that in spite of her being the most incredible, most perfect human being to ever live, with all those obstacles gone, he now stood a chance.

But even having prepared himself so thoroughly for Marcy Hanlon's return to Endicott, Indiana, after fifteen years, Max Travers was in no way prepared for Marcy Hanlon's return to Endicott, Indiana, after fifteen years. He might as well have been a high-school sophomore again, the way he became paralyzed the second he saw her. Even though she was half a block down and on the other side of Water Street, looking in the display window of Barton's Bookstore on a luminous Sunday afternoon in September. But here he was, stopped dead in his tracks, feeling like he'd walked through a time portal.

And Marcy didn't even look much like Marcy anymore. Shoulder-length auburn curls had replaced the stick-straight, strawberry-blond mass that cascaded to the middle of her back when they were teenagers. The alabaster skin she'd had to slather with SPF 50 then was now a sun-kissed gold. A flowing tunic and wide-legged pants the color of summer sage draped her body in place of the ripped skinny jeans and crop tops she used to wear, and gigantic designer sunglasses covered her eyes—eyes he remembered were the pale, perfect blue of a Himalayan poppy.

But even with all the changes in her and the distance between them, Max knew it was Marcy. He knew by the way she had her weight shifted onto her left foot while her right was tipped upward, toes pointing toward the sky. He knew by how she had one hand cupping the back of her neck, a gesture he'd recognized back then was a product of anxiety. He knew by the confident posture that completely contradicted that anxiety, because Marcy Hanlon had always thought she had to uphold the Hanlon aura of perfect family harmony, even though perfect, never mind harmonious, was the last thing the Hanlons had ever been—save for Marcy, of course, since she herself was already perfect in every way.

And he knew by the sizzle of heat that sparked through him, making him feel as if every cell in his body was about to explode. She'd had that effect on him whenever the two of them came within a football field's length of each other. It was just some weird awareness of her he'd always had, even if he couldn't see her, that told him Marcy Hanlon was *there*. There was some strange, irrefutable link between them, as if they'd been matched at the dawn of eternity and tethered together with some cosmic thread that defied all outside efforts to slice through it.

Oh, yeah. Max was definitely feeling the teen angst again. He should probably go right home and scrawl down some slushy "Ode to Marcy," as he had done on a fairly regular basis when he was a kid. He'd really been hoping he'd moved beyond the cringe years, but he supposed they never left a person entirely.

Because the way he was standing here now really wasn't that much different from the last time he'd seen her, waving to him from the rear window of her father's Escalade as the Hanlons passed him on this very street, tailing a flotilla of moving vans carrying everything they owned. It had been the week after their last day of sophomore year, and the realization that Max might not ever see her again had settled into the pit of his stomach like a lump of ice. That impression had only been hammered home when her mother, seated beside her, realized who Marcy was waving to and jerked her daughter around to face the front of the car. Mrs. Hanlon had then thrown Max the most malevolent look he'd ever had thrown his way. And the Hanlons—all of them but Marcy—had thrown him some pretty malevolent looks when he was a kid.

Now he watched as she strode into the bookstore, vanishing from his sight the same way she had that day fifteen years ago. Back then, there had been nothing Max could do about her disappearance. He could no more have followed her than he could stop a sunflower from turning with the sun. Besides, what was he supposed to have said to her back then if he could have followed her? Provided her family would even let him get near her? Anything beyond "Oh, hey, Marcy, wassup?" had rarely ever left his mouth when they weren't in class together. Today, though…

Oh, who was he kidding? He was no more confident in his ability to be suave around Marcy now than he had been then. He should just do what he'd always done when faced with an opportunity to talk to her outside their school environment—turn tail and run.

No, he told himself. No way. He'd been waiting a long time for this day. This was the year Bob was going to make his wish come true. The comet had already granted the wishes of his two best friends, Chance and Felix. The three boys had all been born in a year of the comet, they'd all made their wishes on Bob's next return and now, for his third pass, the big ice ball was making good on those wishes. Chance had learned just this morning that he would be getting his million dollars in the not-too-distant future, and Felix had gotten his "something interesting" a couple of months ago in the arrival of his mysterious next-door neighbor. Why shouldn't Max be rewarded, too? All he'd wished was that Marcy would see him as something other than the kid who took care of her parents' lawn. Yeah, okay, as the now-owner of the landscaping company he used to work for, he still took care of people's lawns. But there was a lot more to him these days than that.

He watched as the bookstore gobbled up Marcy, unable to stop the smile that curled his lips. They'd run into each other from time to time at Barton's when they were kids, and even more often at the library, as both of them were relentless bookworms. So often, when he'd gone to the Hanlons' to work, she'd be sitting poolside reading something. A couple of times, Max had actually stoked up enough courage to ask her about her book, and the two of them would begin a nice chat about it. Until one of her parents or brothers came out the back door to remind Max he wasn't there for a book club and to get back to work.

It was a fair cop. But the real reason the Hanlons had chased him off had nothing to do with his landscaping obligations and everything to do with keeping him away from Marcy. The Hanlons were nowhere around now, though. None of them had ever returned to Endicott after they left. Max could talk to Marcy all he wanted, provided she was up for a chat, too.

Decision made, he headed up the street.

Marcy Hanlon pushed her gigantic sunglasses to the top of her head, gazed at the tall stack of hardbacks on the table in Barton's Bookstore and tried not to cry. Marcella Robillard's most recent mystery novel, *The Devil You Say,* had a reasonably good title and a cover that was absolutely gorgeous—an art-deco-style drawing of a flapper in profile, her heavily lined eyes closed, her red lips parted over a long cigarette holder. The novel had been given Marcella's biggest print run yet, Marcy knew, and the publisher had put buckets of money into promoting it. It had been in the front window of every bookstore the week of its release, and, at this point, it still should have been face out in the mystery section of the store. In some reviews, Marcella Robillard had been compared to Agatha Christie and Dorothy L. Sayers. Her latest cozy should have shot straight to the top of every bestseller list out there. Both she and her new book should still be performing extremely well.

Instead, barely six months after its release, it sat veiled in dust on a remainder table at the back of the store. It hadn't even sold a quarter of its printing, and the only top-ten list it had appeared on, at number ten, had been one for a tiny weekly paper in a tiny coastal town in Maine, where Marcella had bought her first—tiny—summer cottage with the advance from her second novel. And that had only been because the elderly owner of the town's only bookstore had a crush on Marcella and insisted that everyone who entered his store buy her books whenever they were released.

Marcy knew all that, too. She knew, because *she* was Marcella Robillard. Almost as if to prove that to herself, she picked up a copy of the book and turned it over. Yep. There she was on the back cover, looking all successful and confident, happily seated at her Renaissance-era writing desk in her office at the castle—yes, castle—where she used to live. Behind her, the windows had been thrown open to showcase the rolling vineyards of southern France beneath a bright blue sky filled with puffy clouds. The famous Robillard vineyards, producer of some of the best cabernet sauvignon in the world.

Marcella Robillard wasn't just some glamorous

pen name Marcy had chosen for herself. It was her actual, legal name. She'd been born Marcella Genevieve Hanlon and became Madame la Comtesse de Robillard after marrying Monsieur le Comte de Robillard—aka Olivier, aka Ollie—six years ago. Though, now that her divorce was settled, she could go back to her own name anytime—at least in her personal life. Not that the name Marcella Robillard was any great shakes in the literary community these days. It might behoove Marcy to start writing under another name, anyway.

If she could ever crawl out from under the writer's block that had been plaguing her. She couldn't remember the last time she'd been able to wring more than a couple of pages out of herself in one sitting—and those pages were never any good. Who knew if she even had another story in her?

She was about to put her book—*her* book, she reminded herself, one of seven that had her name on it, so she must have another in her somewhere, if only she could find it—back on the table. But the bell above the front door of the bookstore jangled merrily to announce another customer, and she automatically looked up to see who it might be.

And immediately wished she hadn't.

Oh, crap. Max Travers. Who she was totally *not* prepared to run into. Not until she could work the situation from the playbook she'd rehearsed in her head a couple of billion times before returning.

Be cool, she told herself as she watched him stride aimlessly to the new-fiction table. It wasn't like this was any kind of big, unfamiliar experience for her. Barton's Bookstore had been a fixture in Endicott since before she was born. She and Max had bumped into each other here a million times when they were kids. He was the only person in town who'd read as much as she did. Though he hadn't much cared for *The Scarlet Letter*, she recalled, thinking about the paper they'd had to write together in ninth grade. He'd had some excellent opinions and insights on it, though, which had vaulted their project to an A from what would have been a solid B if she'd had to write it alone.

Funny, that, she thought now. Every one of her books had topped a hundred thousand words, and nearly every one of them had made an appearance on the *New York Times* bestseller list, three of them breaking the top ten. But she'd needed Max's help in ninth grade to finish a five-page essay on a book that had already been written.

She'd needed his help with other things, too, back then, she recalled now, the memories pushing to the front of her brain before she could stop them. She'd needed his kindness and his sweetness and his shy little smiles in the hallway. He had no idea how much those smiles had meant to her on days when everything in the world seemed like it was crumbling to gravel at her feet.

How could he have betrayed her the way he did back then?

She needed more time before she was ready to talk to him. She needed to better prepare herself. It was only her first full day back in town. She'd hoped to have a couple of days, at least, to reacclimate herself to the place where she'd grown up before she had to face him. It had just been so long since she was in Endicott, so long since she'd been Marcy Hanlon. She wasn't sure she even knew how to be Marcy Hanlon anymore. Unfortunately, he was standing between her and the exit, and by the leisureliness of his movements, he didn't look as if he was going anywhere anytime soon.

He'd always been like that when they were kids, never seeming to have a care in the world. She used to sneak peeks at him out her bedroom window whenever he was there with Mr. Bartok to take care of the garden. He'd taken his time with the plants, appearing to have a soft spot for each one of them, but he'd always managed to finish his work on time. At school, he was always the last to rise from his desk at the end of class and would amble

casually to the next one. He never wolfed down his
lunch like the other boys. Ironically, he'd lettered
in track and always made the state finals, but not
because he was a runner. He'd been their discus
thrower and shot-putter, always taking his time
to ready his shots, and often winning as a result.
Max had just been a thoughtful, gentle, decent kid.

Which had made it all the more shocking when
she learned the truth about him. That Max Travers
was nothing but a common thief.

Be cool, she told herself again as she watched
him move casually from one table to the next. He
couldn't find out yet that she knew what he'd done
to her family. She had a four-step plan in place,
and she would execute it perfectly. Step one: pretend nothing between her and Max had changed
since they were kids, save those things that were
an inevitable and normal part of growing up. Step
two: lull him into a false sense of security that everything between them was *ju-u-ust fi-i-i-ine* and
see how much she could get him to inadvertently
admit what he'd done fifteen years ago. Step three:
once she had him where she wanted him, smack
him hard with the revelation that she knew he was
the one who'd stolen a fortune's worth of jewelry
and documents from their home. And step four…

Okay, so she hadn't quite figured out step four

yet. She supposed it depended on his reaction to her revelation. First things first. Step one. Nothing had changed since they were kids. However, as she watched Max step into a splash of sunlight streaming through the front window of Barton's, she realized a lot had changed since they were kids. At least where he was concerned. As handsome as he'd been as a boy, as a man… He was staggering. His hair was longer on top, thick coils of black falling carelessly over his forehead and temples. The late-afternoon light streamed over his brown skin, gilding his luscious cheekbones and the biceps that strained against his polo shirt. He'd always had great arms, thanks to the physicality of his job. But he'd been pretty lean otherwise when they were kids, and not much taller than her. He'd grown at least a half foot since then, and biceps weren't the only muscles straining against his shirt. Broad shoulders tapered to a slim waist, all of it solid rock.

She remembered how much she'd always wanted to run a hand over the length of his arms and shoulders when they were kids, because the bumps and curves of muscle were so different from her own scrawny frame. But she hadn't braved even the smallest touch. There had been something about Max that made her feel like, if she touched him, even once, she'd never want to be separated from him, never want to be her individual self again, at a time when she didn't even know yet who her individual self was.

She bit back a derisive chuckle. As if she knew who her individual self was now. She'd reinvented herself so many times since leaving Endicott that she was more foreign to herself than ever.

Max looked up then, his gaze immediately connecting with hers when he saw that she was staring at him. Then he smiled. Oh, god. He smiled one of those sweet, gentle smiles he'd gifted her with in the hallways at school. In an instant, Marcy was fifteen again. But only the good parts of being fifteen. The fun of shopping for earrings at the mall or eating school lunch outside when the weather turned warm. The delight of choosing an outfit for the next day or downloading new music. The breathless excitement of wondering what adventures would come on any given day. And the absolute, joyful ignorance of how the world really worked and how the people living in it truly were.

Max lifted a hand in silent greeting, and something inside Marcy exploded into glitter and cotton candy. Oh, she was so not ready to see him yet. She closed her eyes, inhaled a deep, calming breath and reminded herself that he was not the boy she'd crushed on as a teenager. More to the point, she was no longer the girl who trusted and saw the best in everyone she met.

When she opened her eyes again, Max was making his way toward her. Her heart hammered hard in her chest, and she hoped like hell he couldn't hear it pounding in his ears the way she heard it in hers. Instinctively, she pressed the book she was still holding against herself firmly, as if that might keep in all the wild emotions that wanted to escape.

Be cool, she told herself for a third time, hoping it would indeed be a charm. Thankfully, she did manage to regain some sense of herself before he stopped a mere breath away. But when she saw the shimmer of affection lighting his eyes, the same slate-blue of his polo, she nearly melted into a heap of ruined womanhood at his feet.

He's a thief, she reminded herself. *He's the reason so much went so wrong in your life.* Oddly, though, this moment somehow felt like the first thing to go right in a very long time.

"Hey there, Marcy Hanlon," he said in a voice that was deeper and richer than the one she remembered. Had she been writing about him, she would have called his voice *velvety*. There was a time when she would have shunned a word like that in her writing, thinking it too flowery. But for Max Travers, it was perfect.

"Hey there, Max Travers," she managed to reply in a voice that sounded steady and confident and nothing at all like how she felt.

For a moment, neither said anything more, only studied each other in silence as if taking stock of all the ways they'd each matured. Marcy had changed—physically, anyway—as much as Max had. Living for five years in the Côtes de Provence had burnished her once-pasty skin, and she'd been dyeing and perming her hair and keeping it shorter since college. She was a bit taller, too, and living in a French vineyard with a Cordon-Bleu-trained chef had filled out her formerly lanky build. She'd lived the kind of life as an adult she never would have dreamed she could have had as a kid, one filled with glamour and adventure and passion. Her experiences, both good and bad, had made her much more accomplished, but also much more complicated.

Usually, she liked herself well enough these days, even if she didn't like where life had landed her. But there were times when she wished she could go back to being that skinny, awkward kid. Not just because those had been simpler times. But because there were so many choices she'd made since then that she now wished she could go back and undo.

Funny, but she would have thought one of those choices she could have made differently would have been falling for Max Travers. But looking at him now, feeling the way she was just by being close to him…

No. She still would have chosen differently back then, she told herself, had she known what she knew about him now.

"It's good to see you, Marcy," he said. "I was wondering if you'd be back in town for Bob's return."

"Wouldn't miss it for the world," she replied.

And she wouldn't. Like Max, she was born in a year of the comet. Like every kid her age the last time the comet came around—including Max, she was certain—she'd made a wish when she was fifteen. It was a wish she desperately needed to come true now. Wild horses couldn't have kept her away from Endicott.

Another awkward moment passed in which they only continued to eye each other with much interest…and not a little confusion. Then Max asked, "So what have you been up to for the last fifteen years?"

Marcy nearly dropped the book she was still holding. Had he asked that sarcastically? Or did he really not know what she'd been doing for the last fifteen years, in spite of a good many of those years being covered in just about every tabloid out there? Not that Max was the type to read tabloids. But unless things had changed, one of Endicott's favorite pastimes was gossiping, so she was confident there had been at least some talk about her here. Hadn't there been? Surely, there had. How could Max not know about her literary successes—um, at least until her most recent book or two—and her wildly scandalized marriage? Even before meeting Ollie, her party-hearty ways had been documented everywhere from *The New York Times* "Society" page to *Radar Online*. How had he not heard about her sensationally disastrous dating history and her husband's philandering and profligacy? For a minute, she honestly wondered if maybe she *had* somehow gone back in time.

Then she looked down at the book in her hands that she still clutched to her chest, cover side out. No, she was firmly standing in the present, more's the pity. Immediately, she set the book down on the table, her publicity photo on the back hidden. Then, just for good measure, she moved to stand in front of it. Max honestly didn't seem to know about her history, she realized with a mix of both amazement and relief. He thought she was still just

Marcy Hanlon, coming back to the town where she grew up, for The Welcome Back, Bob, Comet Festival that had been the highlight of their youth.

"Well, let's see," she began, struggling to figure out how she could be honest without telling him the truth. The last thing she wanted him to know about was what a failure she had been at…oh, everything. "I, um, I majored in English at Barnard and then, after graduation, I, ah, worked a lot of different jobs."

Which was true. Let no one ever say a degree in English made a person unemployable. Before selling her first book, Marcy waited tables, tended bar, worked in a lingerie boutique and did some freelance copyediting. She'd had a lot of jobs.

"And then," she continued quickly, "I lived in Europe for a little while."

His beautiful blue-gray eyes widened at that. "Wow. That's pretty cool. What did you do there?"

Again, she struggled to find the right words. No wonder she had writer's block. She couldn't even craft an effective evasion, let alone a novel. "Well," she said again, "I, um, I did a lot of things."

Also true. She had traveled extensively. She had partied with the rich and famous. She had spent more money than anyone should be allowed to have on things no ordinary person needed. And she had watched her entire life go up in flames.

Finally, she said, "Mostly, I worked at a vineyard."

Again, true. She just didn't mention the work she did while working there was writing, not stomping grapes. Marcy hadn't had anything to do with the operation of Robillard Vineyards. That had all been left to her husband. Which went a long way toward explaining why Robillard Vineyards had gone bankrupt in the first place.

Max looked impressed nonetheless. "Boy, you've done a lot more with your time since high school than I have."

Maybe she had. But she'd bet dollars to doughnuts his time had been spent a lot more wisely.

"So how have you been doing since high school?" she quickly interjected, grateful for the opportunity to change the subject.

He lifted one shoulder and let it drop, making the snug cuff of his polo hitch higher. The gesture revealed the hint of a tattoo beneath, another surprise that made her want to know more about his current self. But only because the more information she had about him, the better placed she'd be to take him down. That was the only reason she was curious about his biceps and triceps. And his deltoids and pectorals. And his trapeziuses. Trapezii? Anyway, whatever the muscles in the neck were called. All of them. Because, like she said, the more info she had, the better.

"I'm really not much different from the guy I was fifteen years ago," he told her.

Right. Six feet of hunka hunka burnin' love wrapped in hot deliciousness, with a velvety voice and a mysterious tattoo, was no different from the mellow, quiet kid who threw her uncertain smiles from the other side of the hall.

"Oh, I wouldn't say that," she replied before she could stop herself. When she saw his surprised— and not a little delighted—smile in response, she hurried on. "I mean, yeah, you're still here in Endicott, but I bet you're not still working for Mr. Bartok after all this time."

"No, I'm not," he acknowledged. "Not technically. I bought Lawn Care by Bartok from him when he decided to retire a few years ago. Now it's Travers Landscaping and Design."

It was exactly what Marcy needed to hear him say to reestablish the anger she needed to feel. He'd probably bought the business in cash, with money he made from fencing the things he stole from her family. Her mother's jewelry had been in the family for centuries and would have come to Marcy someday. The stolen documents would have exonerated her father of a crime he didn't commit. She was determined to get it back—all of it, come hell or high water. One way or another, Max Travers would admit to what he did and tell her what he'd done with his plunder.

And one way or another, Max Travers would pay.

Chapter Two

The minute Max told Marcy about buying Mr. Bartok's business, the temperature around them seemed to plummet, and she went visibly stiff. He might as well have just told her he'd spent the last fifteen years abandoning kittens in dumpsters. And she was so nervous. She'd been nervous since he'd looked up at her and made eye contact. Why was she so nervous? He was supposed to be the one who felt on edge and uncertain, standing in the presence of such luminosity and perfection as he was. He was supposed to be the one not sure how to answer her questions. But Marcy had evaded every effort he'd made to get caught up with her, had just glided over what sounded like major life experiences as if they were nothing.

Just what exactly was going on with her?

He reminded himself that they'd never exactly been best friends or anything, so he shouldn't be surprised she hadn't run up and embraced him and started gushing. As nice as that would have been. But she'd always been nice to him when they were kids, and she'd never seemed nervous around him. The last time he'd seen her, she'd been smiling at him and waving. Then again, he hadn't heard a word out of her since the day she left Endicott. Not in person, anyway. They'd stayed friends for a while on social media, but in the middle of her sophomore year at Barnard, she'd suddenly closed her accounts on every platform.

Over the years, Max had tried googling her from time to time, to see what she was up to now, but the only hits had been for other Marcy Hanlons or from the years before she left town. An article about Endicott High School's girls' JV volleyball team going to the state finals. A photo of her and her family when her father cut the ribbon on a new office building he'd built in New Albany. Her taking fourth place in some riding competition in Indianapolis when she was fourteen. There had been nothing about her as an adult.

Which was weird, he couldn't help thinking now. Pretty much everybody landed somewhere on the internet in some capacity, no matter who they were. And the Hanlons had always been such a high-profile family when they'd lived here. Why wouldn't the same be true of them wherever they went afterward? Fifteen years ago, that would have been San Francisco, where, sure, they would have been much smaller fish in a much bigger pond. They still wouldn't have been financial slouches. Their lifestyle should have barely changed. Certainly there should have been some trace of Marcy and her family *some*where since then.

He wanted to ask her if she had time to grab a coffee or something, to catch up on old times, but she suddenly took a step to her right and gestured toward the bookstore exit.

"It's been great seeing you, Max," she said a little breathlessly, "but I really need to bounce. I have to, um…" She paused long enough to let him know that whatever she said next would almost certainly be untrue.

Sure enough, she hurried on. "I have to, ah… I have an appointment with, um, the historical society. Yeah, that's it. To talk about the house."

Right. The massive Hanlon estate that had sat on the hill outside of town with a For Sale sign for years after the family moved away. No one in town had been in the market for such a gargantuan spread. No one in town could have afforded it, other than the Hanlons. And what reason was there for anyone that wealthy to move *to* Endicott? The only reason the Hanlons had been there was because they'd been there for generations.

But because of the house's historical significance—it had been standing for nearly two centuries—and because it eventually must have become clear to Mr. Hanlon that no one would ever buy it for market value, the Endicott Historical Society had scraped together enough money to buy it for half that amount and turn it into a reasonably successful attraction as a historic home and inn. It was a regular stop for school field trips, both here and in neighboring counties, and it was a popular spot for couples to hold their weddings and receptions, then spend their wedding night, before heading off on their honeymoons.

And, to this day, Max still tended the grounds and gardens. Only now, it truly was a labor of love, because the society gave him carte blanche as to what to plant in exchange for the donation of his time to do it. Max ensured everything growing there was local and would have been around in the days when the house had been built. The garden was a lot less showy now, but it was authentic and still quietly beautiful.

He wondered what Mr. Hanlon would have thought about his former home being such a public place now, full of the wretched refuse touring around, gawking at his study and bedroom. He'd never allowed anyone to cross the threshold unless they came from a very specific background. A background few people in Endicott could claim. Max would bet no person of color had ever been in the place during the old man's time. Probably not before then, either. Except, of course, for the ones that had been owned by the family once upon a time.

"My parents still try to stay involved with the place," Marcy continued as she inched away from Max, "even though they don't own it anymore. I promised my mother I'd check in on everything while I was here."

Max didn't doubt that. Of course the Hanlons would want to keep their grip on something that once belonged to them, even if that thing was no longer theirs. What he doubted at the moment was that Marcy really did have an appointment then to do that.

But he didn't push it. Much. "Maybe we can get together while you're here," he said in spite of her withdrawal. "Catch up on old times and every-thing."

Which was actually the last thing Max should want to do. Old times between him and Marcy were a soup of both hope and fear, of both interest and confusion, of both good and bad. What he really wanted to do with Marcy was move forward. The way she was acting now, however, that wasn't looking likely.

"Sure," she said as she continued to make her way toward the exit. "That'd be fun. I'll see you around."

And then, before he could say anything else, Marcy was fairly diving through the door and hurrying past the front window, as if she couldn't escape him fast enough. It happened so quickly, Max could almost feel the breeze on his face as she fled. And it wasn't exactly a warm one.

That evening, at his home—a mostly renovated farmhouse a few miles outside of town—Max cleaned up after dinner and went upstairs to his home office. His speckled mixed-breed rescue mutt, Sodo, named after the town where his mother grew up in Ethiopia, loped along behind him. She took her usual spot, lying atop his feet as he sat down at his desk, her mottled gray fur soft against his ankles. He'd intended to work on next month's schedule for the handful of people who worked for him year-round. Instead, he pulled up his favorite search engine.

It had occurred to him as he spoke with Marcy earlier that, although he'd googled her from time to time over the years, he'd never bothered to look for info about any other members of her family. Mostly because he'd never cared much about any other members of her family. Tonight, though, he was suddenly curious. Maybe learning about the other Hanlons would give him some insight into where Marcy had been over the years. He hovered the cursor over the search box, then began to type her father's name. *Lionel Remington Hanlon*…and, what the hell… *IV.* Not that there could be more than one of them, he was sure. Much to his surprise, though, there wasn't a single mention of Marcy's father in any of the hits that came up. Max tried putting the name in quotes.

No results found.

Okay, that was superweird. He tried different variations of the name within quotes. But there was nothing with Marcy's father anywhere on the internet. Not even a mention of the office building in New Albany that had come up a few years ago when Max searched for Marcy. She had mentioned her parents in the present tense today, so the guy

must still be around. And even if he wasn't, there
would have been an obituary somewhere. A pretty
lengthy one, at that. Max tried searching for info
about Marcy's mother, LuEllen Hanlon. A handful
of hits came up about her being on a fundraising
committee for a children's hospital in San Francisco. But there was nothing more recent than a
decade ago.

Maybe the elder Hanlons had retired and dropped
off the grid, Max thought, to hide out with their
filthy lucre on some secluded island somewhere. So
he tried a different tack. He typed in Marcy's oldest brother's name and found Remy easily enough.
He was running an investment firm in Providence,
Rhode Island. Her other brothers popped up immediately, too. Percy was an architect in Miami, and
Mads was the executive vice president of a bank in
Seattle. None of their professional bios mentioned
a word about having any other family members,
though. No wives. No kids. No nothing.

Maybe that was just a thing in the big-business
community, Max thought. Maybe it was considered
unprofessional to mention you had a life outside
of your job. Maybe. But digging a little deeper—
mostly in the hope of finding some reference to
Marcy—Max learned that Mads did indeed have
a wife. She was a member of the board of direc-

tors at some tony private school. And Percy and his wife had paid more than two million dollars for a painting at some auction, while Remy was involved in competitive yachting with his teenage son. But not a word about any of the brothers in relation to Marcy or their parents. Or each other, for that matter.

Again, superweird. But then, the Hanlons had never seemed like a close-knit bunch. To put it mildly.

He tried searching Marcy again. Nothing. Clearly the only way he was going to be able to find out, in detail, what she'd been doing for the last ten or fifteen years was to ask her in person again. And hope she didn't go all cool and indifferent, as she had today, and then run off as if he was a stranger she wanted nothing to do with.

Then again, he was pretty much a stranger to her these days. And she was a stranger to him, in spite of the fantasy life he'd built for the two of them when he was a teenager and continued to revisit from time to time to this day. The one where they got married straight out of high school, and he opened his own landscaping business, and she wrote the Great American Novel, the way she'd always said she was going to do someday, and he joined her on her book tours around the world, where they also visited all the best botanical gardens. With their kids. All four of them. Who were totally doted on by their grandparents on both sides of the family.

Hey, he'd said it was a fantasy, all right? No way would Marcy's parents have wanted anything to do with any offspring that might spring off him, even if they were half-Hanlon. Hell, *especially* if they were half-Hanlon. All the Hanlons that had come before them would have been spinning in their graves if they knew one of their descendants was anything but Plymouth-Rock white.

Max rose from his desk slowly, so as not to disturb Sodo, who was now snoring softly in a chair near the open window. Then he launched himself into a full-body stretch—he'd been sitting for a lot longer than he realized. When he checked the time on his phone, he was surprised to discover it was approaching midnight. He never stayed up this late. His days at the nursery generally started before dawn and ended at dusk, meaning he'd be lucky to get three or four hours of sleep tonight, especially now that his brain was swimming with questions about the Hanlon family. Or, at least, one member of the Hanlon family. He still didn't understand why Marcy had been so cool toward him that afternoon. Maybe she'd smiled a time or two, but they hadn't been like the smiles she used to throw his way. He was surprised how much he had missed Marcy's smile, even after all these years.

He couldn't wait to try to rouse one again.

Marcy was having trouble sleeping, despite having been exhausted when she finally fell into bed in her room at the Hanlon House Historic Home and Inn. In spite of her ambivalent feelings about her former home's fate, she hadn't been able to resist making a reservation when booking her return to town—though she hadn't exactly anticipated winding up in the room that used to belong to her brother Percy. And sleeping wasn't the only thing she was having trouble with. She was also having trouble with dreaming. Because she'd just awoken from one about Max that she would just as soon not have had, thankyouverymuch, mostly involving her efforts to find out more about the tattoo under his shirt sleeve…and then find out even more about other things under his other garments.

She rolled restlessly onto her side and punched up the pillow, trying to focus on the September breeze drifting through the open window. Outside, a great horned owl hooted in a nearby tree, a sound she remembered well from her childhood. Nothing else about the house was familiar, how-

ever. Although the historical society had furnished
it with period pieces similar to what she recalled
from when her family lived here, they were *different* period pieces. The rooms had been painted
paler colors, more appropriate for the time the
house had been built, and the rugs on the hardwood floors were cotton American-folk style, not
the rich, jewel-toned wool Persians from her memories. The bowling alley and movie theater in the
basement had been returned to being the root cellar and coal storage they once were. The tennis
courts were gone, and the pool had been filled in
and sodded over to make the place more authentic.

When this was Percy's room, it had been filled
with models and LEGO creations, not milk glass
and local pottery. There had been posters on the
wall for Linkin Park and Muse, not oil paintings of
hunt scenes and ornate gold mirrors. Percy would
be appalled if she told him. Not that that was going
to happen, since none of the Hanlon siblings had
spoken a word to each other in more than ten years.
That was what happened when the family patriarch,
who had ruled them all with an iron fist, dropped
such a bomb on them when Marcy was still in college—that he was headed for a seven-year stay in a
federal penitentiary for stealing millions of dollars
from his clients and business partners. And that

virtually every cent he had to his name would be lost because he had to pay them all back.

It was a crime he'd never committed, he assured them, but he had no way to prove his innocence. The reason for that was the documents that would have cleared him had been stored in a portable safe that was stolen from their home in Endicott a few years earlier. Her father had kept their most important belongings in something that could be easily grabbed and taken to the basement with them whenever there was a tornado warning, which happened with some regularity in southern Indiana. What he hadn't considered was what an easy target it would be for a thief.

Also stored in that safe, he was sorry to tell Marcy, was all the heirloom jewelry that had been passed down to the Hanlon women over generations. To make matters worse, the thief who put them all in this spot was the fifteen-year-old boy they'd entrusted to care for part of their home— Max Travers. They had him on security video roaming around the house one day when he'd snuck in unobserved and uninvited. A few days later, when Marcy's father went to remove something from the safe, the whole thing was gone.

Clearly, Max had stolen it, he further charged, since no one other than family had been in the house recently. Unfortunately, they didn't have any video of him actually stealing the safe or carrying it around, which was why they never reported the theft to the police—a reluctance on their part that Marcy still wasn't sure she understood, since they'd been so certain of Max's guilt. But it had to be Max, her father concluded. No other explanation made any sense. And now he—and by extension, the rest of the family—would be ruined.

Her brother Remy had done his best to ensure that that last one, at least, didn't happen, however. He'd been the only one of the children who had enough money to pay a service to scrub every reference of Lionel Remington Hanlon IV from the internet and anywhere else his name might show up. But Remy had done that, she was certain, more for himself than for their father or the family. He shared a name with the elder Hanlon, after all. He didn't want there to be any reason why someone would think Remy was the perpetrator, even if their father was entirely innocent.

Marcy turned to her other side and punched her pillow again, harder this time. The owl hooted once more, and she tried to focus on the soothing sound instead of the unsettling thoughts tumbling through her brain. Instead, she found herself wondering what her old bedroom looked like now that it was bereft of her Harry Potter Funko Pops and Build-a-Bear plush toys. Nothing about her childhood home was reminiscent of the half of her life she had spent there. Which maybe, in a way, was kind of fitting.

She rolled onto her back and stared at the ceiling. Nothing much in Endicott was reminiscent of her childhood, really. Sure, some of the shops on Water Street that she remembered were still there. But Barton's Bookstore had rearranged its shelves and done away with its music section entirely, and there was a coffee bar at the back that hadn't been there before. The ice-cream shop next door to it had newer, trendier flavors. The waitresses at the diner wore jeans and Deb's Downtown Diner T-shirts now instead of the retro waitress livery they used to wear. None of those places was the way she remembered them. None of them was the same.

But she wasn't the same, either. And neither was Max. Marcy may have come home again, but this wasn't her home anymore. Nor was Côtes de Provence. Or Manhattan, where she'd lived when she was in college, and where she'd been couch-surfing with what few friends she still had there since leaving France a year ago. And San Francisco seemed so long ago now. But it had never felt like home. She'd been too raw during the time she spent there, still missing the place where she grew up and all the friends and familiarity she'd left behind in Indiana.

She shook her head. Marcella Robillard would be ashamed of Marcy Hanlon preferring small-town Indiana over the thrill of a buzzing metropolis or European countryside. So Marcy told her to please just be quiet and let a girl get some sleep.

Marcy was still a little dream-hungover and haunted by visions of Max when she went downstairs for breakfast in the room her mother had always referred to as "the salon." Back then, it was a room she'd only seen used when her parents were hosting parties, or on Christmas morning, when the loot from Santa for the four Hanlon children had been enough to satisfy the population of a small sovereign nation. Now it was dotted with tables covered in white linen and filled with strangers enjoying the generous continental breakfast buffet. Her mother would be horrified. But Marcy had to admit the croissants looked delicious.

She filled a plate and was lucky enough to sidle up to a table just as its occupants were leaving. A busboy quickly cleared the used dishes, and after a quick thank-you, Marcy set her phone on the table next to her plate to read the morning headlines. But it was only a moment before a pair of heavy work boots poking out from under faded blue jeans entered her line of vision beneath the table. Presumably, they belonged to someone who expected her to share because it was a four-seater she was hogging to herself. Fine. She'd share the table with a stranger in a room where she'd once had free rein to do whatever she wanted.

When she looked up, however, it wasn't a stranger who had approached the table. Well, not a literal one. It was Max, who had also filled a plate with pastries and fruit and held a steaming mug of coffee. In addition to the boots and jeans, he was wearing a sage-green T-shirt bearing the logo for Travers Landscaping and Design. It was just light enough in color, and just snug enough in fit, that she could make out luscious bumps of muscle beneath. It was all she could do to keep herself from reaching out to strum her fingers along every one of them.

She suddenly felt overdressed in her sky-blue tunic and striped palazzo pants. Though, admittedly, that wasn't really the reason she was thinking about taking them off. In a word, *Ahem.*

"Mind if I sit down?" he asked a little sheepishly.

He did the one-shoulder-shrug thing again, an action she could recall now from their youth. His shirt sleeves today were too long for her to make out even a tiny bit of the tattoo she knew lingered beneath one of them. But that wasn't the reason she was thinking about taking his clothes off, either. *Ahem*.

"Place is pretty crowded," he pointed out unnecessarily. "Not many places to sit."

"Of course," Marcy said, gesturing toward the chair across from her. "I didn't realize you were a guest here?" she added when she realized the significance of his appearance. "Are you not living in Endicott anymore?"

It seemed a ridiculous question in light of the fact that he had a business here, but maybe someone else managed it for him, and he lived somewhere else now and was only in town periodically. She'd simply assumed he was still a resident. She couldn't imagine Endicott without him.

"Oh, I still live here," he said as he settled into his seat. "I bought the old Lambert place out on Route Forty-two a few years ago and have been fixing it up."

Marcy knew the farm well. Everyone in Endicott did. The whole Lambert family had been regular fixtures at the Saturday farmers' market when she was a kid. And, during peach season, she'd often gone to the farm with her mother for fresh peaches.

She recalled that the house had been pretty run-down back then, but there had been a lot of land surrounding it. The property couldn't have come cheaply. Just another example of Max profiting off the things he'd stolen from her family.

She bit back her anger and strove for a light-heartedness she was nowhere close to feeling. "I remember the Lambert farm. Are the orchards still there?"

He nodded as he speared a strawberry with his fork. "Peaches and apples, both."

"Must be a lot of work trying to run a business and a farm."

"Oh, I don't farm the land," he told her. "Nothing's been planted since Mr. and Mrs. Lambert retired and moved to Arizona to be closer to their daughter. I'm rewilding the place."

"Rewilding?" she asked. "What's that?"

"It's letting the forces of nature return the land to its natural state over time. I just leave it alone and let it do its own thing, including the orchards. And they're still thriving pretty well all by themselves."

"What happens to all the fruit? Does it just rot?"

He looked at her as if she'd just sprouted a third eye. "Of course not. I wouldn't let all that delicious-ness go to waste. Everybody in town knows they can come out and pick whatever they want when there's fruit on the trees." Now he smiled, igniting little fires deep in Marcy's midsection. "That's a perfectly natural way to manage the land."

"You just give all the fruit away?" she asked incredulously. Maybe he couldn't get rich off a few dozen trees, but there was still money to be made with them.

He seemed confused by her response. "Sure. I can't eat all that. The gate's always open for whoever wants to come out."

Well, that wasn't very greedy or horrible of him. And he had to be greedy and horrible, considering what he'd done to her family.

She forced her mind back to the matter at hand. "Then what are you doing here eating breakfast?"

"I always have breakfast here before I go to work here. Perk of the contract I signed with the historical society."

It took her a moment to understand. "You still take care of the grounds."

He nodded. Then he smiled again. Marcy tried not to spontaneously combust. Then, softly, he said, "I still take care of your garden, Marcy."

Heat bubbled inside her. But all she said was "It was never my garden. It belonged to my father."

"I don't know," Max said. "You sure seemed to spend a lot of time in it. I still think about you sometimes when I'm there. And I've planted more of the flowers you liked best."

How did he even know what kind of flowers she liked? She'd never even given them much thought.

"There are more lobelias than there used to be," he continued, "because the Gibraltar azaleas your dad insisted on having near them aren't great to grow here. The soil's too acidic. And the ash trees can't survive here anymore with the emerald ash borer, so I replaced them with more pink dogwoods. All the exotic plants are gone, in fact. The historical society wanted the garden to have plants that were indigenous to the area and time when the house was built, and I was totally on board with that. I planted more sweet william, too."

The more he spoke, the more Marcy's mouth dropped open. He was right, she recalled now. Her father may have been superstrict about how the garden looked and was laid out, but he'd never forbidden any of them from going in there, as long as they didn't run wild and make a mess of it. Marcy remembered now how much she'd liked to read there. On a bench near the lobelias. Or in the shade of the pink dogwood. Both of which she had always loved. And the sweet william? She'd been charmed by their colors and always picked one to tuck behind her ear whenever she was near them, being careful to remove it before she went back inside so her father wouldn't know of her transgression.

How could Max have remembered all that when she hadn't even remembered it herself until he reminded her of it?

As if reading her mind, he said, "I remember a lot of things, Marcy. And every time I come here to work, they all come tumbling back."

She shook her head slowly. The way he was looking at her now, over the rim of his coffee cup, his smoky gray-blue eyes full of...something... Something she told herself she shouldn't try to figure out, because the way he was looking at her now...

He sipped his coffee slowly, savored it, then lowered the cup back to the table. And never once did his gaze leave hers. A tsunami of feelings began churning inside her, spinning faster and faster until she began to feel light-headed. Thankfully, he finally looked down at his plate to stab a chunk of pineapple with his fork, and the moment was gone.

"So what brings you back to town?" he asked as he lifted the pineapple toward his mouth. "Is it just the comet festival? Or is there another reason?"

And why did he seem to have an ulterior motive

with that last question? And if he did, then just what, exactly, was that motive?

Oh, what the hell, Marcy thought. She might as well just go ahead and tell him why she was back in town. Not the real reason, of course. Not the part about unmasking his thievery and making him pay. And not the part about needing the wish she'd made when she was fifteen to come true. She'd just tell him the pretense she'd created, the one she planned to tell everyone in town who asked about her return so that no one would question her true motives. The one that she was kind of halfway thinking she might actually do.

"I'm writing a book," she told Max. "About Comet Bob's regular visits to Endicott and the wishes he's granted over the years. And I'm hoping it sells like hotcakes."

Chapter Three

Max was surprised by Marcy's announcement, even though he knew he shouldn't have been. Back when they'd worked on their school essay together, she'd talked a lot about how much she wanted to be a writer someday. Then he wondered why she hadn't started writing before now, especially since she'd studied literature in college and, from what he'd learned about her during their conversation yesterday, seemed to have been living a life for years that would have been conducive to that. He guessed, like so many things in life, the timing just had to be right. And with Bob returning to the place where she grew up, it made perfect sense for her to start writing now and tell the comet's story. He kind of wondered, too, why no one else had done it before now.

"That's a great idea," he said. "You're the perfect person to do it."

She smiled at that, but there was something a little strained in the gesture. She still seemed to be nervous about something, still didn't seem to want to let him get too close. And something told him it wasn't just because the passage of time had wedged too much space between them.

"Thanks," she said. "I thought so, too."

When she didn't elaborate, he asked, "Is it going to be fiction or nonfiction?"

She opened her mouth to reply, but hesitated. Then she closed it again and reached for her coffee. After a thoughtful swallow, she finally said, "I'm not sure yet. At first, I thought nonfiction. Talk about the comet's history and my own experiences with Bob's last return when we were fifteen, and how it is or isn't different this time. I was going to interview other comet kids who were born before us about what it was like for them in their day and whether or not their wishes came true. And I figured I'd talk to some of our classmates about their experiences and wishes last time and whether or not they came true this year.

"What did you wish for fifteen years ago, Max?"

Although Max should have seen that question coming, it threw him totally off-kilter.

Yeah, no. There was no way he was going to tell Marcy that. Mostly because—duh—he didn't want her to know how he felt about her, then or now. But also because no one had ever really decided whether or not revealing the wish diminished its possibility of coming true. Sure, he and Chance and Felix had all always known what each other wished for. But that was because they were best friends. None of them had ever told anyone else what they wished for, save Chance's older brother, who was pretty much just an extension of Chance. Now Both Chance and Felix had seen their wishes come true in one way or another. Max hadn't yet. So he wasn't going to jinx it by telling anyone anything.

"I'm not saying," he said, hoping his smile was mysterious and not miserable, the way it felt.

She nodded, her own smile perceptive. "Meaning your wish hasn't come true this year."

"Not yet," he countered. "But the festival isn't over for another week. And the year isn't over for more than three months." Then he turned the tables. "What did *you* wish for, Marcy?"

Her smile dropped and she dodged his gaze. "I'm not saying, either."

This time, Max was the one to nod. "Meaning your wish hasn't come true, either."

"Not yet," she echoed, reestablishing eye contact. "Like you said. There's still time."

He suddenly wanted very much to know what Marcy wished for fifteen years ago. What did a girl who already had everything ask a wish-granting comet to bring her? She hadn't needed money or friends. She hadn't needed good looks or good fortune. So she couldn't have wanted any of those things. Just what had a fifteen-year-old Marcy Hanlon wanted back then? Max couldn't begin to imagine.

"Well, if you need any help with your book, let me know. Chance and Felix both got their wishes granted already."

This revelation seemed to both surprise and delight her. "Really? How?"

"Chance wished for a million dollars, which he recently inherited from his brother."

Marcy sobered. "Oh, wow, I didn't realize Logan passed away."

"No one did until a couple weeks ago," Max told her. "He left town before Chance graduated and never made contact with anyone again. Chance also inherited Logan's two kids."

"Double wow. That must be a life-changer for him."

"Definitely," Max agreed. "Felix and I are going over to his place tonight to meet them. They have a temporary guardian with them for now, but Chance is going to be on his own after she's gone." He grinned. "He's trying to convince the guardian to stay in town for a while longer. Though that may not be entirely just because she's good with the kids."

"So what did Felix wish for?" Marcy asked.

Max's grin broadened. "He wished that something interesting would happen in Endicott."

Marcy chuckled. "Oh, now that must have been a *really* tough one for Bob to grant."

She wasn't exaggerating. As nice as Endicott was, and as much as Max had always loved living here, it had never been the most exciting place in the world, comet festival notwithstanding. It hadn't even been the most surprising. Or, you know, the most interesting.

Max said, "A couple months ago, a woman came to town and bought the storefront next to Felix's restaurant."

"And in what way is that interesting?" Marcy asked.

"She's easily the most interesting woman in the

world. She's a Rhodes scholar, and a sharpshooter who qualified for the Olympics, and a former aerialist for Cirque du Soleil. She climbed Mount Kilimanjaro… The list goes on and on. Also, Felix has developed a major thing for her."

Marcy gaped at that. "Felix Suarez? The guy who never dated a girl for more than a month when we were kids? The guy who, if memory serves, was in fact stringing along three girls at one time the last time I saw him? And none of them minded about the others?"

"That's the one," he assured her.

"How many girls is he dating now?"

"None," Max said with a laugh. "He hasn't dated anyone since Rory moved in next door."

"Not even Rory?"

Max shook his head. "Nope. She wants nothing to do with him."

Marcy sat back in her chair, clearly impressed. "That *is* interesting."

"So you might want to talk to them about your book."

"I definitely will, if I keep it nonfiction."

"So you might write a novel then?"

"Like I said, I don't know yet. It could make for a good story."

A moment followed in which neither of them

seemed to know what to say next. So they only
nibbled at their breakfast and studied each other
in silence, each seeming to find their meal way
more enjoyable than it actually was.

Finally, after Marcy had finished the last of her
croissant, she asked, "So what else has changed in
Endicott since I was last here?"

Max wanted to tell her that everything had
changed after she left. Because, for him, at least,
everything had. Despite the fact that the two of
them hadn't been particularly close, nothing had
really felt right without her in town. There had
just been something…different. About everything.

So he lied and told her, "Nothing, really. I mean,
your house, obviously," he amended, gesturing
around the room. "And me buying Mr. Bartok's
business and the Lambert farm. And Chance has
a house now, too, in the same neighborhood where
your friend Amanda lived when we were in school.
Felix's grandmother passed away a couple years
ago, so he's taken over the restaurant, and that's
going really well—he's won some big awards. There
are a few new shops on Water Street that weren't
there before. Kickapoo Park is now named after
Mrs. Barclay's late husband, but everyone still calls
it Kickapoo Park. They tore down the drive-in and
built a spa there…"

He stopped when he saw Marcy smiling again. "What?" he asked.

"So, actually, a lot has changed," she pointed out.

Yeah, okay. Maybe a lot had changed in Endicott since they were teenagers. Just not the things Max had needed to change. Like his feelings for the only girl he'd ever...had a thing for. The essence of the town and its people were still the same.

Then he realized that no, that wasn't exactly true, either. The spirit of the town and its people *had* changed after the Hanlons left. It had improved without her father's arrogance and his disdain for everything and everyone that wasn't like him weighing it down. And without her brothers' menacing and bullying, things at school had improved, too. But Marcy's absence...

Well, no good could come of it when the one perfect thing to ever exist in Endicott drove off in the back of an Escalade, never to be seen again. Or, at least, not for another fifteen years.

"Um, yeah, okay," he agreed. "A lot has changed. A lot more hasn't."

She looked as if she wanted to change the subject as well. Instead, she said, "You've changed a lot, too, Max."

He had no idea why she would think something like that. He'd changed least of all.

"I haven't changed," he assured her. "I'm still doing the same job. Still hanging out with the same guys. I still dress the same and listen to the same music. I see my family practically every day and have dinner with them once or twice a week."

I'm still in love with the girl I've always loved, he silently added, making himself finally admit that. He did love Marcy. He'd always loved Marcy. How could he not? She was everything that was good in this world, all rolled up into a gorgeous package of perfection. Ever since he'd seen her standing outside the bookstore yesterday, his whole life felt centered again after being off-kilter for more than a decade. Honestly, he was more himself now than he'd been in a long time.

Marcy shook her head. "No. You've changed."

"In what way?" he challenged.

But she only smiled a cryptic little smile and said, "You're taller. Your hair is longer. You have a tattoo."

He glanced down at his left arm. How did she know about that?

"I noticed it yesterday," she said, reading his mind. "Your sleeves were shorter. I couldn't tell what it was, though."

That last comment was punctuated by an expectant look, but no way was Max going to push up his sleeve and show her. Because the tattoo on his left deltoid was a tangle of lobelias. Chance and Felix had razzed him so hard about the flowers after getting it that he'd gone back to the tattoo artist a week later and had himself inked with a more "masculine" snake plant on his left trapezius. And, man, if guys didn't get over their hang-ups about thinking flowers were feminine things, then they were going to keep missing out on a lot of cool scientific…stuff. Not to mention, flowers were some of the most sexual creations on the planet.

"You've changed, too," he said, deflecting the conversation from himself.

She deflated a little at the change of subject. But she only replied, "Yeah, I know."

"New hair, new clothes, new way of life."

"Those are just the obvious ones," she told him.

He could tell immediately she regretted saying that. Her eyes widened in something akin to panic, and she dropped her gaze back to her now empty plate, staring at it as if willing it to produce something else for her to eat so that she'd have a reason for not talking. But there was no chance was Max going to back down after a statement like that.

"What are the less obvious changes?" he asked her.

Instead of answering, she glanced at her phone. "Omigosh, is that the time?" she asked in a way that made him think she wasn't even trying to disguise the fact that she was ending this conversation now. She looked back up at Max, standing to collect her things as she did. "I have *got* to get going. It was great seeing you again, Max. I'm sure we'll run into each other again this week. Enjoy your day."

And then, before he could say another word, she was bolting from the table toward the exit.

Later that evening, Max and his friends Chance Foley and Felix Suarez were sitting around the firepit in Chance's backyard, finishing off the last of the beer. It had been a weird night. Chance's newly acquired niece and nephew, both six, were clearly going to be, uh, a bit challenging. He was going to have his work cut out for him, learning to be a dad to both. And the capable temporary guardian with them, a Poppy Somebody, seemed no more able to control the kids than Chance was. She sure was cute, though, Max had to admit, if you went for the cute and cautious kind. Which, when he thought about his two interactions with Marcy so far, he guessed he kind of did.

Except it wasn't Poppy he'd spent the evening thinking about. And now that she was in the house helping put the kids to bed, Marcy swirled around in his head even more.

"So what's this book Marcy Hanlon is going to

write?" Chance asked as the flames in the firepit dwindled to a few whispery flashes around the base of the wood.

They'd spoken briefly earlier in the evening about developments in town due to the comet festival, Marcy's return being one of them. But they hadn't been able to go into much detail about anything, because Chance's niece, Quinn, had dug up a grub and needed information about it *now*. And since Max was the resident expert in all things that came out of the ground, he'd been the one to provide it.

Now he told his friends, "She said it's about Comet Bob's visits to town and the wishes he's granted in the past. Don't know if it's going to be fact or fiction, though. She kind of talked like it could be either."

"I'm sure it'll be fiction," Felix said. "Is she going to write it under the name Marcy Hanlon or as Marcella Robillard?"

The question confused Max. Especially when Chance reached over and smacked Felix against the back of his head. Hard.

"What?" Felix asked, rubbing his head as he threw Chance an indignant glare.

Chance's eyes widened theatrically, and he tipped his head silently toward Max. Felix continued to look irritated for a few more seconds, then his expression changed to one of dismay.

"Ai, dios mio," he muttered to Chance. Then he turned to look at Max. "Forget I said that, *mijo,* okay?"

"Said what?" Max replied. "Who's Marcella Robillard?"

"Dammit, Felix," Chance said through gritted teeth.

"What?" Max demanded.

His two friends exchanged another cryptic glance, then, as one, turned to look at Felix.

"Marcy has been writing books for years," Chance said. "Mystery novels. Some of them have been on the *New York Times* list."

That had to be wrong, Max thought. He would have heard about that. And there would have been a million hits for that whenever he googled her. He told his friends exactly that.

"She doesn't write under Marcy Hanlon," Chance said in response. "She writes under the name Marcella Robillard."

How did Max not know any of this? Especially since Chance and Felix obviously did. "So… what?" he asked. "That's her pen name?"

Chance looked at Felix. Felix looked at Chance. Chance shrugged. Felix shrugged. Then they looked at Max again.

"Not exactly," Chance said. "Her real given name is actually Marcella."

"How do you know that, but I don't?"

"She sat behind me in first grade," Chance told him, "when I had Mrs. Hazlett, and you and Felix were in Ms. Nguyen's class. When Mrs. Hazlett first started taking roll, she called out, 'Marcella Hanlon?' After a couple weeks, though, Marcy started asking to be called Marcy instead."

"It was kind of a big name for a little girl," Felix said philosophically.

Chance nodded sagely in response.

"So where does the Robillard come in?" Max asked.

There went his friends' cryptic glances again, followed by the return of their attention to Max.

"Robillard is her married name," Felix told him.

What? Max thought. *"What?"* he exclaimed. "She's *married*?"

Why hadn't she mentioned a husband on either occasion when he'd seen her? He tried to remember if she'd been wearing a wedding ring, but couldn't recall. He hadn't exactly been looking at her hands. Not with a face—with eyes—like hers. Was her husband here? And if he was, why hadn't he been with her? And why had Max never heard about her getting married? What the hell was going on?

"Just tell him everything," Chance said to Felix. "Now that she's back in town, he's gonna find out at some point, anyway. We can't keep this quiet any longer."

"Keep what quiet?" Max asked. "There's more? Her being a bestselling author and married isn't enough?"

Felix inhaled a deep breath and released it slowly. He drained the last of his beer and set the bottle on the patio beside his chair. Then he said, "Marcy is kind of famous."

"Anybody who follows celebrity culture knows her," Chance added.

Which explained a lot, since Max had no interest in anything related to the entertainment industry. He didn't go to movies much, watched very little TV and mostly listened to the music he'd been listening to since he was a teenager. He read a lot, but he hadn't read any mysteries since high school. He liked adventure and history. He didn't even recognize Marcy's bestselling-author name.

"I mean, that makes sense," he said in response to Chance's statement. "If she's a bestselling author and everything."

"No, even before she sold her first book," Felix explained. "When she was at Barnard, she dated one of the more notorious Kennedys and ended up in the gossip magazines a lot. I guess he was kind of her entry into that lifestyle, because she dated a lot of guys like that afterward and showed up in the gossip magazines even more."

"There was that soccer player from Munich," Chance said. "What was that guy's name?"

"Jürgen Günther," Felix said. "That guy was at his prime when she started dating him, but he never played well again after she broke it off. And there was that sculptor with one name. Cremora or something."

"Cosima," Chance said, correcting him. "His art went down the drain after she split with him. And that astronaut?"

"Scooter Bundersen," Felix said in a rueful voice. "Man, no one has seen him since he wandered into the desert after Marcy dumped him."

"At least she married the count," Chance said.

Max's head was spinning. Marcy had broken the hearts of a soccer star, an artist and an astronaut? She'd married a count?

"Holy crow, her husband is a *count*?" he asked his friends, hating that he suddenly sounded all of fifteen years old again.

"Yeah," Chance replied. "Her husband is Oliver Robillard, a French count who owns some swanky vineyard."

"*Olivier* Robillard," Felix corrected him. "And he's only a viscount."

Only a viscount, Max repeated to himself. A *French* viscount. Holy crow.

"But he is French," Chance pointed out. "His family makes the wine with the castle on the label."

Felix nodded. "The wine that's so expensive, I don't even carry it at La Mariposa. No one here could afford it. And the castle is the family home. It's where he and Marcy live when they're in France."

At this point, Max was reeling. The girl he'd loved since high school lived in a French castle by some French vineyards with a French viscount. On some level, though, that all made sense. It was the perfect way to live for a perfect person like Marcy. Of course, she would have ended up in an amazing place like that. In an amazing life like that. One filled with beauty and excellence and brilliance. Just like her.

And she was married to the French viscount, he reminded himself, something he'd been trying not to think about. Marcy was married. But that shouldn't surprise Max, either. Of course a luminous woman like her would be married—she'd obviously had to fight the guys off, after everything Chance and Felix had just told him. And of course she would be mar-

ried to someone like a French viscount. That was…
Well, that was just perfect.

"Why didn't you guys tell me all this?" Max
asked, still dumbfounded. "For that matter, why
didn't anyone else in town ever mention this to me?"

"Look, Max," Felix said. "Everybody in Endicott knows how you felt about Marcy when we
were kids. Everybody in Endicott knows how you
still feel about Marcy as an adult."

"How does everybody know that?"

"Oh, for God's sake, Max," Chance said. "The
logo for your business is a dogwood tree that has
MT plus MH equals heart carved into it."

"Not to mention," Felix added, "that when you
go to the website for the business, the services are
listed in order as 'Maintenance, Aeration, Recla-
mation, Cultivation, and Yardwork,' which is just
an acronym for Marcy."

Damn. Max had meant for those to be little Eas-
ter eggs that only he knew about. He'd told the
graphic designer to make the initials in the tree too
small and indecipherable to be noticed by a casual
observer, and he'd thought she'd done a great job
with it. Clearly, he'd been wrong. Then another
thought struck him. He'd been wearing his Travers
Landscaping and Design T-shirt when he ran into
Marcy at breakfast that morning. Had she noticed?

In spite of the evidence to the contrary, he said, "But the initials are so small in the logo, no one can see them."

"They can if they look at it long enough," Chance said.

"And also if Ivy Clutterbuck notices it and tells everyone in town, so now everyone in town talks about it," Felix added.

Crap.

"Look, it's fine that everyone knows you still have a thing for Marcy after all this time," Chance assured him. "It's kind of sweet, really, when you think about it."

It wasn't sweet when Max thought about it. It was pretty frustrating. And now that he knew everyone else knew, it was also pretty mortifying.

"Okay, so maybe we didn't tell you about Marcy's comings and goings over the years," Chance conceded. "We didn't want you to get hurt."

"And, okay, so maybe we didn't let anyone else in town tell you, either," Felix added. "Maybe we reminded them all how much it would break your heart to know what was going on, and since everyone here loves you, they agreed to keep their mouths shut. So sue us."

"We did it out of love," Chance assured him, Felix nodding sympathetically at the same time.

Max had no idea what to say in response to that. He didn't doubt for a moment that his two friends had only been trying to protect him. It was something they'd been doing for each other since they were kids—hiding the ugly truth about reality when things went wrong or, at the very least, spinning it all in a way that helped them get through it. But this? Marcy dating celebrities and marrying a French viscount? Marcy becoming a celebrity herself? How was he supposed to compete with all that? He'd been fantasizing for years about how impressed she was going to be if she ever came back to Endicott and saw how he could grow her favorite lobelias all year round. *Outdoors.* But all this? And the fact that she was married?

No way was Bob going to be able to fulfill his wish this year. Max would be lucky if Marcy gave him more than the time of day. No wonder she'd seemed nervous and distant, and hurried off every time he tried to talk to her. She'd probably needed to get back her husband, the French viscount.

Then he remembered he hadn't exactly been specific in his wish to Bob fifteen years ago. All he'd asked was that Marcy see him as something other than the lawn boy. Chances were good that Bob had indeed already fulfilled Max's wish. Now Marcy was probably seeing him as the most pathetic excuse for a human being that ever existed.

"I gotta get going," he said to no one in particular. "I need to go home and..."

What? he asked himself. Have another beer? Do some laundry? Pretend today never happened? Drink hemlock?

"I need to go home and get some sleep," he finally said.

That much he was sure was true. Not that he was convinced he'd get a wink of it. And tomorrow...

Man, oh, man. Tomorrow—and every day after it—he would just focus on making sure he never saw Marcy Hanlon, or Marcella Robillard, again.

In spite of his assurances to his friends that he needed sleep, the moment Max got home, he went straight to his office, pulled up the search engine on his desktop and typed in the words *Marcella Robillard*. This time, there were more than a million hits on Marcy's name. The vast majority were about her books, but some were about her, interviews she'd given to different industry publications or newspaper articles about her when she'd visited different cities and towns for promotional reasons. He scanned some of those, but her replies to questions asked of her generally gave away very little of her personal life, other than the things he'd been told by Chance and Felix. Then Max clicked on *images*, and there she was, in a number of photos of different social occasions, some from the time before she was married or published. The reason those hadn't shown up when he googled her before was because she evidently started going by Marcella Hanlon when she went off to Barnard.

So Max typed *Marcella Hanlon* into the search bar, and wow... Talk about personal. There were even more photos of her, going all the way back to her college days, virtually all of them featuring her on the arm of some impossibly handsome guy or B-list celebrity. Marcella Hanlon had obviously enjoyed her first taste of life out from beneath her parents' thumbs. A lot.

There she was, dancing at a nightclub in New York City called Provocateur. And another in Las Vegas called XS. And one in LA called Avalon. And... Wait a minute. Was that Orlando Bloom she was dancing with? Holy crow. In addition to all the pics of her at nightclubs—and there were plenty—there were others of her at a host of private functions where she was clearly enjoying herself. A lot. She even showed up on a handful of red carpets. But what caught Max's attention the most was that in nearly every photo of her out partying,

Marcy looked totally different. Her hair changed color and length constantly. In some pictures, she was wearing a lot of dramatic makeup, while in others, she looked like she was wearing none. Her clothing went from skintight and bright neons to conservative, nondescript black, to the soft, flowy pastels she seemed to favor now. It was as if she had gone through years of constantly changing everything about herself that she could. And then…

Then Max saw the photographs from Marcy's wedding to the viscount. The guy couldn't have looked more perfect. Blond, blue-eyed, built. Dressed in a perfectly tailored suit with perfectly tailored looks. Clearly a man who had never dirtied his hands or any other body part. A man who could hold his own in any social setting and knew which fork was for the shrimp cocktail and which glass was for the dessert wine. In other words, he was the complete opposite of Max. That was who Marcy had chosen to spend the rest of her life with. Seeing her standing beside him in a white dress that had a train flowing down the steps in front of them, and a crown of white ranunculus and gypsophila… He couldn't help the sigh that escaped him. She just looked so beautiful. So radiant. So… So perfect.

He sat back in his chair and stared at the collage

of photographs on his computer screen for a long time. None of the women in any of the pictures looked like the Marcy he used to know. Not even the one from her wedding. But none of them looked like the Marcy who had returned to Endicott this week, either. Just who the hell was she now? he wondered. And why, suddenly, did he want to see her even more badly than before? So much for his earlier promise to himself about avoiding her. He honestly couldn't wait to find her again.

Chapter Four

Tuesday morning found Marcy sitting on a bench near the lobelias in what used to be her father's garden—not the bench the Hanlons had owned when she'd lived here, but a different one that was more historically accurate—staring at the open notebook on her lap. Or, more specifically, staring at the blank screen of the open notebook on her lap. At the beginning of her career, she could pound out more than three thousand words before noon, so enamored had she been of the written word and the act of putting as many as she could down on paper. These days, she was lucky to have a few hundred words by then. And even at that, she often deleted them all to start over again. So far this morning, she'd managed to type exactly twelve words: *I was born in Endicott in a year of the comet, and.* Oh, but hey, there was a comma in there, so that at least brought her character count to thirty-nine. Yay. The more she looked at those characters, though, the more she hated every one of them.

Why couldn't she write?

Her first book had flowed from her fingertips and had taken less than six months to complete. She had just married Ollie and was newly arrived in France, and she'd been overcome by the enchantment of her new marriage and the magnificence of her new surroundings. That first book, *The Secret of the Silent Sommelier*, had come to her as easily as it would have had someone been whispering the story into her ear. She'd felt more like she was channeling it than creating it. Her second book, *The Case of the Careless Cooper*, had gone even more smoothly, making her feel as if her continuing protagonist, ex-patriot wine heiress, flapper and amateur sleuth Daisy Cargill, was her new best friend. And when her third book featuring Daisy, *The Mystery of the Missing Maître d'*, had been optioned for a major motion picture—which, okay, never actually materialized—Marcy had felt like she was set for life. She'd had it all planned. She could write a book or two books a year, watch them climb the bestseller lists, option them to Hollywood for some ungodly amount and add to her and Ollie's already vast wealth.

Unfortunately, midway through her fifth book, *Title to Be Decided*, she discovered she was living with The Treachery of the Terrible Two-Timer. Except that it was nothing like the cozy mysteries she wrote and everything like the overblown, overwritten, over-the-top potboilers she did her best to avoid. And Ollie wasn't just two-timing her. He was eight-timing her. And he was spending more money than he had a right to spend. Certainly more money than the two of them had. Not only had he speculated, invested badly and gambled away his own money, he'd lost Marcy's, too. But it wasn't until the bank came to foreclose on the castle that she knew about any of it. He'd already been toeing the bankruptcy line when she married him—which, of course, Marcy had known nothing about—and it hadn't been long before *everything* was gone. Including Ollie.

They had split nearly two years ago. That fifth, only half-completed book had to be finished by a ghostwriter, but the person had done a pretty good job with the bones that Marcy had gotten down.

Good enough that *The Villainy of the Vicious Vintner* had sold comparably to her previous titles. Unfortunately, the book after that, which had been under contract to her publisher before everything fell apart and had to be written quickly to capitalize on her snowballing success, had had to be entirely conceived and composed by a ghostwriter, because Marcy's creative well had gone dry. But that writer hadn't put any of the usual Marcella Robillard touches into the story. Daisy Cargill became a Roaring Twenties caricature, and her father's vineyard in the Loire Valley might as well have been located in Lubbock, Texas.

Determined to turn both her career and her life around, Marcy had been hell-bent on writing the latest Daisy Cargill mystery herself. Delighted that she was returning, her publisher decided that *The Devil You Say* would be a jump-starting do-over with a new direction for Marcella *and* Daisy. Her title and cover art were both dramatically different from those of her previous books. Marcy developed a whole new storyline for Daisy, who took over the running of her father's vineyard, and at the end, finally got engaged to her sweetheart, Armand. That last plot point was something Marcella's readers had been begging to see after years of the will-they-won't-they teasing she had written for them.

But as desperately as she had wanted and tried to get the story down on paper—or, at least, the notebook screen—Marcy's efforts to do so had been terrible. Her writing had been bland and awkward, and it had taken her three times as long to finish that book as the others. After she finally turned it in, her editor told her they would need to send the manuscript to a book doctor to "tighten it up." Pretty much publishing code for a rewrite. And although the young man promised he was an absolute fan of the previous books and swore he knew Daisy better than anyone except Marcella herself, he hadn't captured any of the wit or color that Marcella had become famous for back when Marcy had been able to write the books herself. And now… Now she couldn't even write bland or awkward. Now she couldn't write at all.

It had been nearly two years since her marriage dissolved, she reminded herself. Even though they'd been years of struggle, with her having to rely on friends to survive, that chapter of her life was over. Her divorce had become final a few weeks ago. Ollie and Provence felt as far away from her now as every other part of her life before them. She should be over all of that by now and firmly entrenched in yet another reinvention of herself. God knew she'd transformed herself often enough in the past that she was an expert at it by now. At the moment, however, it was starting to look like this latest reinvention was going to be The Downfall of the Destitute Damsel. Or The Wrecking of the Woebegone Wordsmith. Or The Liquidation of the Lackluster Loser. Or The—

"Hey, Marcy."

She closed her eyes as something uncomfortable lodged in her chest. And now, here was Max, just when she'd been thinking she had reached her nadir. But no. There was more. Now the man she was determined to prove was a thief would be witness to The Reproach of the Rock-Bottom Writer, and that would make it even worse.

When she looked up, she couldn't make out his features because he was backlit by the early morning sun, making her squint and shade her eyes with her hand. He seemed to realize the trouble his position was causing, so he took a step to his left, until he was blocking the sun from her eyes. Not that that really helped, because not only was he now standing closer to her, but he was also surrounded by an aura of gold that bathed his dark skin in warm amber and placed her firmly ensconced in his shadow, a realization that made her feel a little...unsettled.

"Hello, Max," she said. "Fancy meeting you here."

Why was she surprised? She knew he worked here and was as fond of the garden as she was, so it was likely she would run into him here at some point. Which, okay, might even be subconsciously why she'd come out here to write this morning in the first place. Because she needed to see him if her plan was going to work. She needed to lull him into that false sense of security and have him believe she was on his side. That was the only reason she wanted to have anything to do with Max Travers. False sense of security. And she was going to get right on it. Starting this very minute.

"Join me?" she asked. She punctuated the question by patting the other half of the bench.

He looked surprised—and not a little concerned, for some reason—by her invitation. But after a moment's hesitation, he took a seat beside her. As far away from her as he possibly could without falling off the bench, she noted, but still beside her. Sort of.

"I didn't expect to see you here two days in a row," she told him.

Now that the sun was no longer in her eyes, she could see him clearly. He was dressed the same way he'd been the day before, in faded jeans and a

T-shirt for his business. But whereas yesterday he hadn't yet gone to work—both he and his clothes had both been pristine—this morning, he'd clearly already put in some time and effort. Dirt streaked both his garments and arms, and a dark spot of something ashy-looking smudged one of his beautiful cheekbones. Perspiration dotted his forehead and darkened the front of his shirt, and she'd be lying if she said she didn't notice the earthiness of his scent. On him, though, somehow it wasn't nearly as unpleasant or off-putting as it had been whenever Ollie came in from inspecting the vineyards. And Ollie had never lifted so much as a finger to perform any kind of physical labor. He'd only strutted around under an umbrella, ordering his employees to do his bidding.

"Normally, I'm only here once a week or so, if that," Max said. "But we're heading into fall soon. There's a lot to do in September. I came in early to plant some spring bulbs and bring some of the potted plants inside the house. I still need to do some pruning and cleaning for some of the others. Cut some herbs for the Hanlon House herbalist to use in her demonstrations for the tourists, that kind of thing."

"Hanlon House," Marcy repeated, trying not to choke on the words. "I still can't believe the place where I grew up is called that now. I can't believe it's a tourist attraction, open to the public."

"I guess it must be weird, seeing that and staying here as a guest."

As if cued by his comment, an elderly couple perusing a map of the house and grounds strode past them, the wife saying something about a bright red cardinal perched in the salvia and the husband responding that he hoped the inn still had apple pie on the dessert menu tonight.

"It's surreal," Marcy said once they'd passed. "I mean, when my folks put it up for sale, I just assumed some other family would buy it, and it would stay private with that family living in it, and be the kind of place I'd drive by with my children someday and say 'See, kids? That's where I used to live,' and then keep driving. To have it so... So open...so available to whoever wants to come in... I guess it belongs to everyone now."

She suddenly recalled how her father used to rage against socialism and how it was going to spell the end for capitalism and the American Way. As a girl, she hadn't known what any of those things were, and she hadn't cared. As a woman, she knew and understood them...and she still didn't care. All she knew was that her home was no longer her home. Which would have been okay, she supposed, if it was someone else's home. But although it might belong to everyone now, that meant it didn't belong to anyone. And that just hammered home her own condition of not belonging to anyone, either.

Not that she wanted to be owned or anything like that. But it would have been nice to belong.

"No one here in Endicott could afford it," Max said plainly. "And any family that could afford it didn't really have any reason to move to Endicott."

"I get that," she agreed.

At the time her parents put the place up for sale, she hadn't been able to understand why her father was so determined to move, since the house had been in his family for seven generations. It had all happened so quickly, too. One evening, over dinner, her father announced to all of them that he was relocating his business to the other side of the country, and they'd be putting the house up for sale and moving after the end of the school year. Which had only been six weeks away at that point. Marcy had barely had time to digest the massive change to her life when it came time to leave Endicott and her friends and everything she'd ever known and loved behind.

And then San Francisco had been the antithesis of Endicott, so huge and fast-paced and alien, she'd never gotten used to living there. Her two oldest brothers hadn't made the move with the rest of the family, because they'd both started college by then. But Mads had still had a year to go in high school—his senior year. He'd been even angrier than Marcy had about the move. And he'd left the West Coast immediately after his graduation to attend college at Notre Dame, where his girlfriend—who was now his wife—had been accepted, too.

None of them had been able to understand their father's need to turn his back on the only place any of them had ever called home. Not until the phone call that came midway through Marcy's sophomore year at college. The conference call between the entire family where her father explained to them all how, even when Marcy was in high school, there had been murmurings at the investment company he owned and operated about embezzlement and theft. He'd suspected as much himself, and he'd realized he could potentially be viewed as the one who was committing it. By then, too, he knew all the documentation that could clear him was gone, because it had been stolen shortly after the beginning of the year.

Although it wasn't his finest hour, her father had told the family that night, he panicked and shut down Hanlon Investments, Inc. in New Albany, and moved everything except his employees across the country. It was an effort to distance himself— both figuratively and literally—from what might be going on at the company he was responsible for. It hadn't been enough, however, to keep the crimes from eventually coming to light. And once they did, years later, he looked to be the mostly likely perpetrator and had no way to prove he wasn't. As a result, the family fortune was about to be confiscated by the authorities, and he was likely on his way to jail.

Then, after that very thing happened, Marcy had wanted to forget she'd ever lived anywhere. She certainly didn't want to be Marcy Hanlon anymore. So she turned into a million other people instead. Party girl. Nerdy girl. Goth girl. Hippie girl. But none of those identities had stayed around for long. And none had made her happy at all.

"It's a really popular attraction, your house," Max said, bringing her back to the here and now. "The place gets bookings for weddings all summer long, sometimes from as far away as Indianapolis and Nashville. And a lot of little kids are learning about history, thanks to this place."

As if that was supposed to make Marcy feel better. To know happy couples were celebrating their love in one of the most loveless places in the state, and that children were learning about a place whose history was fraught with oppression, from the time it was built until the time she and her family moved out of it.

"That's great," she said. It was a lie, of course. Because the last thing she wanted was for Max to know what a miserable existence she was living these days. Or what a miserable existence she'd had as a kid. Her father's list of rules for the rest of the family had been endless.

When she looked at him again, he was eyeing her with much interest, none of it seeming good. Enough that she couldn't help saying something.

"What?" she asked.

He inhaled a soft breath and released it. "So did you bring your kids to Endicott with you to show them where you used to live?"

It was an odd question, and she wondered why he would even ask it. Oh, right. Because she'd just mentioned doing that with her children. The ones who didn't actually exist. He must have misunderstood.

"I don't have any kids," she told him. "That part was hypothetical."

"How about your husband? Did you bring him?"

Marcy's heart sank at the question. Especially when Max continued.

"You know. The French viscount? Who lives in a castle with you?"

Something cold and wet slammed into her belly. Someone had gotten to him since yesterday. She wondered what else they had told him about her.

"Ollie and I are divorced," she said softly, cautiously. But she didn't tell him anything more.

She wasn't sure, but she thought she saw a flash of relief skitter through his eyes. Even so, he said, "But you're still wearing your wedding ring."

She looked down at the third finger on her left hand. She did still wear her wedding ring. Mostly because it was made of platinum and had been designed and handwrought by one of Europe's most sought-after jewelers. It was worth quite a bit, and the way things had looked when she left Provence, she'd feared there would come a day when she would need to cash it in because she'd simply exhausted every other revenue source she had. She still feared that. Plus, it didn't really look like a traditional wedding ring, since it was fashioned to look like entwined grape leaves. Then again, the fact that she wore it on the finger she did could easily signify that a wedding ring was exactly what it was.

Without giving it further thought, she twisted the ring from her left ring finger and moved it to her right.

"So then you're not married?" he asked, as if wanting to make doubly sure he'd heard her correctly about the divorce.

She sighed with resignation. She really didn't want anyone in Endicott to know what a shambles her life had become. She'd been so careful to live out of the public eye after everything that happened in France. As far as she could tell, all of her friends still living in Endicott thought she'd been leading an exciting, glamorous life since leaving town, and that she was still a huge success in both her career and her social life. Not that she'd actually seen any of her friends that still lived here. She'd done her best to avoid all of them and had succeeded so far.

Well, except for Max. But he wasn't exactly a friend, was he?

"I only keep the ring on because it's valuable," she said. "And I don't want to lose it for the same reason."

What little money she had left was going fast, after all, with most of what was left being spent to stay here, in what was once her own home.

She told herself to make clear to Max that she was the one who'd wanted out of the marriage. But it wouldn't have been long before Ollie made the same decision, once he finished running through her fortune as quickly as he had his own. He would have needed another cash cow who could maintain his excessive lifestyle. So, instead, she said nothing more.

"Anyway," she continued, "Ollie and I haven't been together for a long time."

She wondered why she felt the need to explain all that to Max. Then she remembered, *Oh, right. To lull him into a false sense of security. That's why.*

Reluctantly, she added, "Things were starting to go sour between the two of us a long time before we separated."

It was a hard admission for her to make. Looking back, she realized things with Ollie had never been as good as she always told herself they were. As soon as they'd moved to Provence from the States, where they'd enjoyed a whirlwind romance of only six months before marrying, things had started going…not well. In hindsight, she saw so many clues that Ollie had been unfaithful from the start and reckless in his spending even before he met her. But she'd been too wrapped up in the joys of writing and the romance of her new life to acknowledge any of that.

"I was the one to finally file for divorce," she told Max. "It just took me a while to come to terms with the fact that I failed at marriage so badly. And at a lot of other things, too." Before he could ask

her to clarify that admission—which she could tell
he was about to do—she quickly said, "Who told
you about my marriage?"

He hesitated, then said, "The real question should
be, why didn't you tell me about your marriage? Or
about living in France. And writing books. And…
and everything else. Jeez, Marcy, I flat-out asked
what you'd been up to for the last fifteen years.
Why didn't you tell me any of that stuff?"

She'd asked herself that very question after she
and Max parted ways on Sunday. Everyone in Endicott must know what she'd been doing since college. Her name and face had been plastered on
every rag in the grocery store checkout lines, and
on every splashy celebrity website on the internet.
Gossip was the favorite pastime of her hometown.
She was amazed that Max had clearly not known
any of it.

Which maybe was precisely why she hadn't
filled him in. Because, for those few moments with
him, she hadn't been Marcella Robillard, disgraced
socialite and literary deadbeat who'd traveled all
over the world and dated some of the most desirable men on the planet and written bestselling novels before going down in flames. She'd just been
Marcy Hanlon from Endicott. For those few moments, she could erase her reality and make up

something fantastical that might have been her lot in life had things turned out differently. If she hadn't stumbled into New York society and met so many glamorous, influential people. If she'd seen Ollie for what he was right off the bat and walked away. If she'd stayed here in Endicott or come back as soon as she could. Her life could have been—would have been—so much different.

In those few moments of talking to Max in the bookstore, her whole world had opened up, and the possibilities for happiness had seemed endless. At that point, even a few moments had been a wonderful gift. A gift she'd wanted to enjoy. Even if it only lasted for a few moments.

But how was she supposed to explain all that to him? And how was she supposed to tell him anything now without giving away that it wasn't just her marriage that was a failure, but everything else in her life, too? Bad enough he knew the truth about her and Ollie divorcing. Marcy had hoped to keep all that a secret while she was here in town. She wasn't sure she could face her former friends and neighbors if they knew how badly she'd mucked things up.

So she just replied, "I don't know why I didn't tell you, Max. I guess…" She sighed heavily and changed tack. "I'm only going to be in town for a week. And I don't plan to see a lot of people. It's just easier if I don't have to explain anything about... anything."

"Meaning you'd appreciate it if I didn't tell anyone about your divorce."

"I would appreciate that," she admitted. "At least until after I'm gone."

He looked at her for a long time without speaking. Then, very quietly, he said, "I won't tell a soul."

Something strangely happy hummed in her chest. Not just because of what he'd promised, but because of the way he'd said it. As if he sympathized with her. As if he understood what it was like when other people talked about you behind your back or didn't really see you for who you were.

"Thanks, Max," she said.

He did the one-shoulder shrug. But not enough to reveal his mysterious tattoo. "No problem."

Right. No problem. Not for him, anyway. Not yet, she quickly amended. She really was going to create a problem for him. She really was going to put him on the spot about what he did before she and her family left Endicott. And she was going to make him pay. Soon. Really soon. Like, within days. Really.

She just had to figure out how she was going to do it.

* * *

Only hours ago, Max had promised himself he was going to stay away from Marcy. But when he'd seen her sitting in the garden in the same place he'd seen her when they were kids, reading with one foot tucked under her leg, the same way she had when they were kids, looking so engrossed in whatever she was reading that she seemed to become part of the garden itself, the same way she had when they were kids...

He bit back a sigh. It had just felt like time was dissolving minute by minute, day by day, year by year, until he was standing in the garden as a teenager, feeling all the same things he'd felt back then. Adoration. Awe. Captivation. Love.

He did love Marcy. He admitted that to himself without inhibition now. He had loved her, probably, since third grade, when she came to his rescue on the playground after her brother Percy coldcocked him upon learning Max had given his sister a valentine for Valentine's Day. This, after the exchange of valentines had been obligatory in Mr. Levy's class so that no one got left out. Meaning Marcy had gotten one from every other kid, too, girls and boys alike. But only Max had been singled out for that transgression, with a roundhouse to the side of his head that had nearly knocked him out.

When he'd come to his senses, Marcy was standing over him looking worried beyond her years, and the smile that shone on her face after he opened his eyes had been like fireworks streaking across the night sky. She asked him if he was okay, and when he nodded, held out a hand to help him up. Then she awkwardly patted him on the arm, spun on her heel, ran to catch up with Percy...and shoved him with all her might.

He went down hard. Then he jumped up fast and turned on his attacker, fist clenched tight. When he saw it was his sister, he dropped his hand to his side. Until Marcy lit into him with a verbal tirade to end all tirades. Then Percy clenched his fist tight again and glared at Max. His brothers had joined him, ignoring Marcy's berating, and glowered at Max.

The threat had been pretty clear. Stay away from their sister, or next time, he'd get pounded by all three of the Hanlon boys.

In third grade, he'd been small enough and timid enough to be cowed. Even with Chance and Felix on his side, no way could they have handled Remy and Percy and Mads, all older and bigger than them. For a long time, he only adored Marcy from a distance.

But he did adore her after that. Always.

And now she wasn't married, after all. He felt like a boomerang. This morning, he'd awoken devastated that Marcy was a married woman. Now she wasn't. That knowledge made him happier than he'd been in a long time. Until he realized it meant she had once loved someone enough to pledge her life to him. Someone who wasn't Max. From what he'd heard, divorces could be complicated, and the feelings around them could be cloudy. Marcy had loved her husband once upon a time. Just because they'd split up didn't mean she'd stopped caring about him. Did she love him still?

"S-o-o-o-o-o…" he began, stringing the single syllable over several time zones. "Do you have a lot of plans for the festival this week?"

He had meant for the question to sound harmless and insignificant, something to jump-start the conversation after it had grown serious enough to make them both uncomfortable. Instead, to him, it sounded like a desperate plea for her to go out with him.

Marcy didn't seem to take it that way, though, thankfully. She looked grateful for the change of subject. "I do, actually," she told him. "They have a lot more going on this year than they did when we were kids. That stargazing in Kickapoo Park tonight with Mr. Aizawa looks pretty interesting. It would be great to see him again."

Mr. Aizawa had been their science teacher in ninth and tenth grades. Max still owed him a debt of gratitude for partnering him with Marcy in lab for a term. Not that Mr. Aizawa realized that, but still.

"How old is he now?" Marcy asked.

Max smiled. "He's still teaching at Endicott High. He's only like sixty."

She looked surprised. "Seriously? He seemed so old when we had him in class. I was kind of surprised he was still around when I saw he'd be hosting the event."

"Everyone seems old when you're fourteen."

"I guess so. Anyway," she continued before he had a chance to ask if she actually planned to go to the stargazing, or if maybe she wanted to meet up there and then go for a bite afterward, "I love that they're doing a lot of the traditional stuff that they did last time, too—the Parsec Picnic, the Big Bang Brunch, the Supermassive Mini-marathon." She grinned. "And, best of all, the Galaxy Ball. I'm really looking forward to that. I can't believe Mrs. Barclay is doing it again this time. How old is she now?"

"Now she is getting up there," Max said. "The

whole town celebrated her ninetieth birthday back in June."

"Wow."

"But she's still going like gangbusters. Still volunteers at the library. Still power-walks through town like a champ. Still likes to take out her little runabout on the river and still goes way too fast."

While Marcy took a few seconds to ponder that, Max seized the moment. "Did you get your invitation to the ball? Everyone in town who was born in a year of the comet gets invited to that thing. They mailed them out about a month ago."

He knew this because his had arrived a month ago. The minute he'd opened it, all he'd been able to think about was whether or not Marcy was somewhere opening hers, too.

"I didn't get it in the mail," she said. "Probably because no one knew my address. I've moved around a lot since leaving town."

Max thought that was weird. Even if she'd moved around a lot, someone in town had to know how to get in touch with someone in her family. Her folks still had friends here, as did her brothers. Surely, someone had stayed in touch with them and could have asked where Marcy was living. Unless no one in her family knew where she was living, either.

"But then I ran into Mrs. Ballard, who helped

organize it, and she handed me one she was carrying in her handbag. I guess a lot of people they haven't been able to locate come back, so they just sort of pass them out when they see us."

Max's heart began to hammer hard in his chest when he realized what he wanted to do. What he was going to do. His palms grew damp, his face felt hot and his brain began to swim a little.

"So…are you going to go?" he asked, hoping he didn't sound as uncertain as he felt.

She nodded. "Of course, I'm going. I wouldn't miss it."

Still feeling uncertain, still hoping he didn't sound that way, still trying not to pass out, he asked, "Got a date for it?"

Now Marcy looked kind of uncertain, too. She hesitated, but not because she was looking for an excuse to turn him down, he didn't think. Instead, she said, a little uncertainly, "Um, no. No, I don't."

Now Max's blood was roaring in his ears, and his heart was thundering so hard, he was sure Marcy could see it slamming against his chest. "Would you like a date for it?"

She smiled. One of those soft, sweet smiles he remembered from high school. "I would, actually. That would be nice. Thank you."

Max smiled back. But all he managed to say in response was "Great."

After that, neither of them seemed to know what to say. For a moment, Marcy only met his gaze shyly, and he could only gaze back.

Then, speaking even more softly than before, she asked, "Do you think you'll go to the stargazing in the park with Mr. Aizawa tonight?"

Max actually hadn't planned for it one way or another. Suddenly, though, it sounded like an excellent idea. "Are you going to be there?" he asked.

She nodded. "I thought I'd get there around eight, since the talk starts at eight thirty."

He nodded back. "Then I'll be there at eight, too."

"Great," she said, echoing his earlier response. "I guess I'll see you there."

"I guess you will."

He was about to ask her where they should meet when both of their phones suddenly erupted with an emergency signal. Max got to his first, then leaped up when he saw what it said. There was a little boy lost in the nature preserve behind Chance's house, and the alert was asking for help from anyone who could spare the time. But it wasn't just any little boy. It was Finn Foley, Chance's six-year-old nephew, for whom he'd just assumed guardianship. Then he realized he'd received a text from Chance more than an hour ago about that very thing, one he hadn't seen because he'd been too distracted thinking about Marcy.

"I gotta go," he told her. He pointed at his phone. "This is Chance's nephew. I need to be out there helping look for him."

"Oh, no," she said, sounding genuinely distraught. "Can I help, too?"

Max shook his head. "There's two hundred acres of woods out there. Anybody who's not familiar with them would get lost, too. I'll coordinate with Felix. But I really do have to go."

She nodded. "Of course. Good luck."

"Thanks."

Without another word—without another thought—Max took off to help his friend. It didn't occur to him until hours later, shortly after he and Felix located Finn safe and sound, that he and Marcy had never mentioned where in the park they would meet at eight. It was right about the time he also realized he didn't have her phone number to text her and ask.

Chapter Five

*H*e's not coming.

That was the only thought swirling through Marcy's head at eight-fifteen as she paced from one side of the main entrance of the park to the other, then back again. She'd learned several hours ago that Chance's nephew had been located and reunited with his family and was doing fine, so she'd hoped Max would still be able to come to the park tonight. Since she didn't have his number to text him, and although there were other ways into the park, this one, she'd figured, would offer her the best chance of crossing paths with him. Now, however, she was beginning to think maybe he'd changed his mind. Not that she blamed him. The day must have been exhausting for him. But she'd still hoped he would make it.

She was surprised by the depth of her disappointment that he hadn't shown. And there was a part of her that suspected the reason for that disappointment wasn't just because this would mess up her plan to get closer to him and expose him as a thief, which was truly why she wanted to see him tonight. It was. She looked at her watch again. Now it was eight twenty. He really wasn't coming.

"Hi."

She spun around to find him standing on the other side of the entrance gate, as if he'd just been created on the spot from a pile of stardust. He was wearing a white camp shirt spattered with midcentury modern starbursts, along with jeans slightly nicer than those he wore to work. In place of the work boots, he was wearing a pair of camel-colored canvas sneakers—no socks—that she couldn't help thinking looked brand-new and somehow didn't quite suit him. What seemed even more out of place was that he was carrying an insulated cooler in one hand and what looked like a small tarp rolled up under the other arm. That suggested picnic. Which, in addition to seeming like a strangely intimate thing for them to do when they were still in the process of reconnecting, didn't look good for the flowered sundress in blues, lavenders and greens that she'd thought would be a good idea to wear.

"Hi," she replied automatically.

For a moment, neither of them said anything—they only stared at the other as if seeing each other for the first time again. Finally, Max took a few steps forward, enough to bring him to within touching distance.

"I got here a little early," he said, "and I had a quick look around to save us a couple of seats. But all the seats in the amphitheater were already full. Guess Mr. Aizawa brings in a bigger crowd these days than he did in freshman science."

"Well, there are a lot of out-of-towners here, too," Marcy pointed out, trying not to notice how the light from the setting sun lit tiny gold fires in his hair or the way he smelled like sage and rosemary. Trying to remind herself that her reasons for being here did not include enjoying Max's appearance or his scent or his company. Even though, after only a few minutes, she was really enjoying Max's appearance, scent and company.

"It never occurred to me to bring chairs," he said, "but I keep a tarp in my truck, so we can sit on that. It's clean," he quickly added when he must have thought her lack of response was due to her concern, when in fact, it was because she was just loving how easy and effortless the sound of his voice was, flowing over her own angst and anxiety. "I washed it like a week ago, after I had to use it for hauling away some underbrush."

He seemed to notice then how she was dressed. "I didn't think about you being in a dress. I mean, I don't think I've ever seen you in a dress."

That was because she'd never worn them as a child or adolescent unless her parents were dragging her to some major event that required one. And, of course, Max never attended any of those.

"Oh, wait, yes, I did," he amended. "Once. At Mrs. Barclay's Galaxy Ball, fifteen years ago." He smiled. "It was blue. You looked really nice that night."

She was surprised—and not a little delighted—that he remembered. But she recalled what he was wearing that night, too. A dark gray suit. Which was something she'd never seen him wearing before, either. And she remembered how handsome he'd looked in it. Even if it was too big and probably borrowed from a cousin.

"You looked nice that night, too," she said, a little breathless. "And I'll be fine in a dress tonight," she added, suddenly fearful, for some reason, that she might say more than she should about that night at Mrs. Barclay's.

And it would be fine. The dress, anyway. It was long, and its skirt was full, and it would be easy enough to manage. Her memories of the party at Mrs. Barclay's house years ago were less fine. Because she was remembering, too, how seeing Max in a social setting for the first time—for the only time—had felt so much different from seeing him in a school setting, and how giddy she'd felt that whole night over everything that was happening.

"What's in the cooler?" she asked in an effort to keep those memories at bay.

He glanced down at it, then back up at her. "I wasn't sure if you'd have a chance to grab dinner beforehand, so I threw together a few things in case one of us gets hungry. Or thirsty," he added almost as an afterthought. "There's some water and a bottle of wine in there, too."

"Wine sounds good," she said. Maybe it would help soothe her rattled nerves.

"I scoped out a couple of potential spots to sit," he told her. "If we hurry, there will probably still be a few places where we can spread out."

They didn't hurry. In fact, they ambled along in soft, meaningless chatter as they made their way to a spot near a trio of redbud trees, where there was still just enough space for them to lay out Max's tarp. Which was actually more like a sailcloth blanket, she saw, as she took the two corners opposite the ones he held and they opened it over the grass. Though, had it been a blanket, it probably wouldn't have covered more than a single mattress. Once they had it flat, and they situated themselves, there was barely six inches of space between them. Max gestured toward the cooler, and when she nodded, he unzipped it to reveal two bottles of water, two plastic wineglasses, a bottle of pinot noir and containers filled with fresh berries, sliced apples, cheese, pistachios and crackers.

"That actually looks really delicious," she said.

"You sound surprised," he replied. But there was teasing in his voice when he added, "What did you think I was going to have in there? Pizza rolls and pork rinds?"

She laughed lightly. "No. Well, okay, yes. Maybe. Or something similar. Most men don't seem all that concerned about their snacks, as long as they're salty and full of fat."

He popped the cork on the wine and reached for one of the glasses. "Nah. I like to keep my eating pretty clean. I'm mostly vegetarian these days."

"Mostly?" she echoed.

"I still can't resist Chance's ribs or my mom's

doro wat. It's an Ethiopian chicken stew," he clarified when he must have realized she had no idea what that was. "Other than those, I steer pretty clear of eating meat."

She didn't know why that surprised her. Max had always been one of the gentlest souls she knew. At least up until she realized what a crook he was, she meant. It made sense that he wouldn't eat living creatures. Though maybe his choice was for health reasons. She somehow suspected it was as much the former as it was the latter. Maybe more.

No, no, she immediately contradicted herself. It had nothing to do with being kind to animals, since that would suggest he was decent, and decency had no place in the soul of a thief. If he ate clean, it was only because he was selfishly protecting his own health.

She ignored the absurdity of that thought and forced her attention back to the matter at hand.

"I don't think I could be vegetarian," she said. "I don't like vegetables enough. They're just so bland."

"People who don't like vegetables have just never had them prepared the right way," he told her.

"If you say so."

"Hey, Endicott even has a vegan restaurant now," he told her. "You should eat there while you're here. Kay's So Raw So Raw."

She laughed at the pun. "Seriously?"

"Yep." He hesitated for a moment, then added, "Maybe we can meet there for lunch before you head home."

"Maybe," she said noncommittally.

Mostly because, after this week, she'd have no home to return to. She'd run out of friends and acquaintances in New York to ask for favors, and she'd barely made any friends or acquaintances as a girl in San Francisco. She'd kept to herself at her new school, counting the days until she could graduate and go back home to Indiana. But she hadn't come back to Indiana—not with an acceptance to Barnard, her dream school, waiting for her. After that, everything seemed to happen so quickly. Her life became so episodic. Then Ollie, then writing, then...

Then failure. Failure so abysmal that she had nothing now. No job. No family. No identity. No home. And no idea what she would do once she checked out of her room on Sunday. It would be like leaving home all over again, except, this time, she had nowhere to go and no one to go there with.

Seriously, Bob, anytime you want to grant my wish, I'm ready for it.

She sent the cosmic nudge skyward just as Max finished pouring her wine. He handed her the glass then poured another for himself. When they tipped their plastic rims together, he softly uttered, "Clink," and then they each sipped. The sun was sinking lower in the sky, and twilight was fast descending. She remembered that when she and Max were teenagers, a big thing for kids to do about once a month was steal a bottle from their parents' liquor cabinets and gather in the park to party. She'd come with her friends sometimes but couldn't recall ever seeing Max there.

She looked out at the tree line beyond the amphitheater, awash in the last rays of violet light. "Remember when we were in high school," she said, "and a lot of the kids would come here on the weekends to party?"

"Yeah, I heard that was a thing," Max said, "but I never really did it myself."

"I know," she told him. "I came from time to time, but I never saw you."

He looked surprised. "You didn't seem like the party girl back then."

His use of the qualifier *back then* didn't escape her notice, and she realized that whoever had told him about her career and marriage must have told him about her college days, too. Not that she was ashamed of any of that. Well, not really. She'd been a kid, and kids sometimes made choices that weren't exactly wise. She'd had a lot to get out of her system when she left home for college. Living with her family, she'd had little opportunity to express herself or be the person she wanted to be. Hell, back then, she hadn't even known what kind of person she wanted to be. The prospect of absolute freedom for the first time in her life had made her woozy with all the possibilities, and she'd gone a little overboard. She'd had a lot of fun living that way for a while. But she'd eventually come to realize that lifestyle wasn't one that suited her.

"I was mostly there just to hang out with Amanda and Claire and some of the other girls," she told him. "I didn't do any drinking. I couldn't abide the taste."

He smiled. "So you *tried* to party, you just couldn't stomach it."

She smiled back. "All right, fine. I tried Mike Wolowitz's jungle juice. Once." She shuddered at the memory. Her throat had burned all night after one sip. "I don't know how that guy escaped esophageal trauma, the way he put that stuff away. I remember Felix and Chance being in the park on those weekends sometimes," she added. "But they didn't really party that hard, either. I always thought it was kind of odd you were never with them. You three were practically joined at the hip when we were kids."

"I had a lot of obligations at home," he told her. "My dad always had to work weekend nights at the bowling alley. And Mom always had papers to grade. Since I was the oldest, I tried to help them out as much as I could, keeping an eye on my sister and brothers."

That was something else Marcy remembered from their youth, too—how close the Travers family seemed to be. Whenever she ran into Max at the library, he was usually there with his parents and siblings, too. And the whole Travers family was always there for school functions as well, like band recitals and spring plays and open houses. Marcy could count on one hand the number of times her own parents had come to school for things like that. And they'd had the same number of offspring as Max's parents had, so it wasn't like they'd been overburdened.

"How are your folks doing these days?" she asked him.

"They're good," he told her. "Dad still owns the bowling alley, though he's started cutting back on his hours. Mom is still teaching at the middle school. I think they're both looking forward to retiring before too long. Now that they've paid off their mortgage, they've started talking about a lot of other stuff they want to do. Hobbies, traveling, spending time with their grandchildren."

"They have grandchildren?" Marcy asked. "What? Did Lilah and the twins get married?"

Max chuckled. "Only Zach. He got married in the spring. But none of us has kids. That doesn't keep Mom and Dad from talking about how much fun they plan to have with their grandchildren. We hear about it at least once a week."

Marcy laughed, too. Her own parents had exactly one grandchild—her nephew, Stephen, Remy's son. He was a teenager now, but Marcy had only met him a handful of times when he was preschool age. Her parents didn't seem to be overly concerned about adding to their collection of grandchildren, though. As long as there was at least one to carry on the family line—and yay, it was a boy, so the name would be carried on, too—they were satisfied. Certainly, Marcy had never felt any pressure from them to procreate. Of course, she hadn't felt much of anything from her parents for years. Or even before then, really.

But they'd been talking about Max's family, not hers. A much nicer topic of conversation.

"So how are Lilah and the boys doing?" she asked.

Lilah, Marcy remembered, was the youngest of the Travers siblings and had still been in elementary school when she and Max were freshmen. Zach and Gabe, fraternal twins, had been somewhere in between.

"Lilah's working on her master's degree in biochemistry at IU South and wants to go for a PhD in epidemiology. Zach works for the Louisville water company as a resource engineer, and Gabe is an environmental scientist. He lives in DC now, working as a pollution investigator for the EPA."

"Wow," she said. "Sounds like the Travers kids are all banding together to save the planet."

Except for the one who stole things from others, she added to herself. Every time she had a positive thought about Max, she would remind herself he wasn't the man he presented to the world. He couldn't be. He was a wolf in sheep's clothing. A poison apple. A Trojan horse. Fool's gold.

She groaned inwardly. This was why she couldn't write. The only words she could conjure these days were ones someone else had already written.

Then she wondered how his parents could have afforded to send three children to college on the salaries of a teacher and a bowling-alley owner. Maybe Max had funded their education with his ill-gotten gains. The jewelry he'd stolen from her parents had been worth millions. He could have more than covered their tuition with that. But then, why wouldn't he have funded his own? He hadn't mentioned going to college himself. Just that he'd bought Mr. Bartok's business from him. Which, yeah, he could have also done with the take from his crime.

Was that why he'd done it? she wondered. To put his family on a better footing? That would be more in keeping with his motives, because he did still seem like a decent guy. That didn't excuse what he'd done, however. Thievery was thievery, regardless of the reasoning behind it, and that was a crime. Even though, yeah, Jean Valjean would probably like to have a word with her at the moment.

But Max had done more than steal from her family, she reminded herself. There had been documents in that safe that could have cleared her father's name, too. Maybe she and her father hadn't always gotten along, but he hadn't deserved to be accused of a crime he didn't commit and spend five years in a federal prison because of it. Lionel Remington Hanlon IV had little more than his name left to him at this point. And that, too, was worthless, thanks to Max. Exposing his crime wouldn't just solve that crime and punish the criminal. It would right a wrong. Maybe Marcy's family hadn't been as close and loving as Max's was, but that didn't mean they should be penalized for something none of them had done. She didn't care if Max's motives were selfless or not. And who knew for sure what his motives had been in the first place? He had, without question, personally benefitted from his theft. And her family had, without question, suffered as a result of it.

He laughed lightly, shattering her musing—the sound was just so warm and lovely and such a direct contrast to the thoughts swirling in her brain.

"I never thought about it like that," he said. "But, yeah. I guess we are, in a way. Mom and Dad instilled a love of nature in all of us. He took us camping whenever he could, and she got us all gardening as soon as we were old enough to hold a trowel. Some of my best memories of childhood are being out in our garden with her, on our knees, digging in the dirt and dropping seeds into it. She'd take us all out every morning before school to tend to everything. Even in the summer, when school was out, she'd wake us up early. And every night when the weather was warm, we'd sit outside admiring our work."

For some reason, Marcy felt herself tearing up as he spoke. There hadn't been a single activity she and her mother had regularly shared together. She wished she could say that was because she was the youngest, so by the time she came along, her parents were both exhausted with the social obligations of the three children that had come before her. But the truth was, her parents hadn't done much with her brothers, either. Even though all three had excelled at sports, her parents never went to the games or meets. Marcy had played flute in every school band recital for years, and she'd been in every spring play. But her parents had never been in the audience for any of them. Her mother would have been horrified by the very idea of being on her knees in a garden, never mind digging in the dirt.

Hastily, she dabbed at her eyes. Max noticed and looked concerned.

"You okay?" he asked.

She nodded. "Allergies, I think. Something must be blooming tonight."

"Primrose," he said easily. Because of course he would know what might be causing her fake symptoms. "And there may still be some tuberose holding on, too. I didn't know you had allergies. They didn't seem to bother you when we were kids. You were in that garden all the time."

That was because she didn't have allergies, then or now. Not that she was going to tell Max that.

"Anyway, sounds like your whole family is doing well," she said, changing the subject.

He nodded, but still looked concerned. Or maybe suspicious. Though Marcy was going to cling to concerned.

"Yeah. They are," he told her. After only a small hesitation, he asked, "How are your parents and brothers doing?"

Her indignation returned at his audacity in asking the question. He even managed to sound genuinely interested in her answer, which couldn't be possible, with or without his having stolen from them. Marcy wasn't stupid. She knew her family had never treated Max well. Her brothers had bullied him on a fairly regular basis when they lived here, and her parents had never shown even a hint of courtesy when he worked at their house. And that all happened long before his theft. Her parents hadn't liked anyone who wasn't a member of their social stratum—and there hadn't been anyone in Endicott who had come close to the wealth of the Hanlons. The elder Hanlons had done the bulk of their hobnobbing in Louisville, across the river, where there had been a handful who could claim the same wealth that they'd accumulated, thanks to the happy luck of their births and marriages. Had there been a tony private school within decent driving distance of town, Marcy was certain she and her brothers would have attended it. Her folks had never made secret their distaste for their children having to mingle with commoners in—gasp—public school.

She had no idea how to reply to Max's question. She couldn't exactly tell him she hadn't spoken to any of her brothers in nearly a decade without explaining why. And she couldn't reveal how seldom she spoke to her parents for the same reason. She reminded herself she made a living as a fiction writer, so she should just make up something that sounded plausible. Then she remembered how badly her career was tanking, precisely because it was impossible for her to tell a story anymore.

Thankfully, someone on the stage of the amphitheater tapped the microphone, and a loud electronic squeal went sailing over the crowd. Marcy and Max both grimaced at the sound, then laughed.

"Wow," he said, "that's exactly what happened in high school, whenever someone handed Mr. Aizawa a microphone."

The crowd went quiet after that, and their old high-school science teacher—who, Marcy was amazed to realize, really wasn't all that old, after all—introduced himself. Then he began to talk about the history of Comet Bob and offered a number of suggestions as to why, every time he returned to Earth, he always made his closest pass to the planet directly above Endicott, Indiana. And suddenly, Marcy recalled that he had given them this very lecture in ninth grade, tailored to interest fourteen-year-olds instead of the general public.

The more Mr. Aizawa spoke, the more she felt like she was back in high school again. Specifically, the semester when she and Max were assigned to be lab partners by the very man speaking to them now. She remembered that first day of school, when Mr. Aizawa had paired up all of the students by literally drawing names out of a hat. They'd all been lined up at the back of the room, and as each set of names came out, those two students made their way to one of the fifteen lab desks lined up in five rows of three. She recalled watching her closest friends, one by one, paired with someone other than her. Then the two cute boys she'd hoped to get to know better had been paired together.

Before long, only four students were left—she and Max, and Iris Fernsby, resident goth girl, and Pez Lambert, the captain of the JV football team. At the time, she'd been hoping she would end up with Iris, mostly because she wanted to ask her how she got her eyeliner to do that thing it did.

She really didn't know Max at that point, beyond his name and seeing him around, and Pez was just so… Pez. She'd held her breath after Mr. Aizawa pulled out her name first, then tried not to be too disappointed to be paired with Max instead of Iris. But she and Max had hit it off pretty well, and right from the get-go, too.

She remembered that on that first day, he'd actually extended a hand and introduced himself to her, even though the school was small enough that everyone at least knew each other by name. Even so, she'd shaken his hand and introduced herself, too. And when he'd replied, "I know who you are, Marcy Hanlon" in a voice that was soft and certain, a weird ripple of…something had gone up her spine. He'd said her name as though it was a benediction. Something sacred, to be uttered with only the utmost reverence. No one had ever spoken her name that way—as if it was special. As if she was special.

More memories fell into her head after that. Meeting him at the library to work on their English paper when they were sophomores, because his house was always full of the bustle and bedlam of loving commotion, and there was no way her parents would have allowed him to come inside her house. And seeing him on Water Street as her family drove out of town to start their lives anew in San Francisco.

She'd been so upset that day. She'd had barely a month to prepare after her father told them all they were leaving town for good. During the entire drive through Endicott, she'd searched out the window of their Escalade in an effort to stamp every detail of the town on her brain and in the hope of seeing her friends just one last time. But she'd only seen Max. He was walking up the street with a bag from Barton's Bookstore under one arm and a milkshake from Deb's Diner in his other hand. She could tell that when he saw the car, he knew exactly who it belonged to, and he'd searched the windows for…her? He must have been looking for her. So she'd waved frantically from the back seat in the hope of drawing his attention. He'd lifted his milkshake in salute, but he'd looked the same way she felt at the time. Then her mother had jerked her around in the seat so she was facing forward again. And then Marcy had started to cry. And she didn't stop until they hit the Kansas state line.

That memory was so vivid still in her brain that, for a moment, she began to feel as if it were almost possible to close her eyes, count to ten, then open them to discover she and Max both had traveled back in time half their lives and were sitting in the park as teenagers. And, oh, what she wouldn't give if they couldn't do exactly that, even if only for the two or three hours tonight would end up being.

What would she do if that was possible? she asked herself. If she and Max could be fifteen again, but still have the knowledge of the world and themselves that they'd earned in the years since? But no. She wouldn't want to do it that way. If she went back in time, she wanted to be as blissfully ignorant of the realities of adulthood as she had been as a teenager. The way she was feeling at the moment, she would give all the money in the world to be able to—

"Marcy?"

Her name sounded as if it was coming from Comet Bob himself, so far away and otherworldly it seemed. Then she realized it was Max who had said it. But when she looked at him, he wasn't fifteen. He was thirty. She wasn't in the past. She was in the present. And something about that made her feel sadder still.

"Sorry," she said. "Must have zoned out for a minute."

"Try an hour," he told her.

"What?"

He lifted his wrist and pointed at his watch. It was going on ten o'clock. Mr. Aizawa's talk was over, and people were filing out of the park to go home. The sky above them had grown dark, and only she and Max were left under the redbud trees.

"I think I missed the whole talk," she said, mystified.

"You were definitely somewhere else for most of it," he told her. "Where?"

No way was she going to tell him that. So she only shrugged and shook her head, saying nothing.

"Want me to recap?" he asked.

Honestly, she wasn't all that keen to hear a science lecture. She'd only decided to come tonight because it was something to do to keep her from having to return to the hotel that used to be her home, because being there just felt so weird. But she discovered, to her surprise, that she honestly wouldn't mind spending a little more time with Max. Even more surprising, her desire to do that wasn't just because of the lull-him-into-a-false-sense-of-security thing. It didn't matter what they were talking about.

So she said, "Sure. What did I miss?"

He sighed. "Unfortunately, I don't have the visual aids Mr. Aizawa had, but I'll do my best."

"What kind of visual aids?"

"A sky chart."

She looked up at the sky overhead. Now that

the amphitheater lights had gone dark, the sky was pretty clear. Certainly, she could see Bob up there winking back at them.

She pointed upward. "What about that sky chart?"

Max looked up, too. "Oh, yeah. Might get a crick in our necks, though."

Marcy lay back on the blanket and gazed straight ahead at the stars. "Speak for yourself."

He stretched out beside her. "I guess it all depends on your perspective."

Perspective, Marcy thought. Yeah, that counted for a lot.

She made herself pay attention this time as he recapped everything Mr. Aizawa had told them— most of which she really did remember from school—then, for a moment, they only lay in silence under the night sky, gazing up at the stars. It truly was a beautiful night, a soft breeze ruffling the leaves of the trees above them, smudges of white and gray clouds drifting across the moon. Comet Bob seemed to be sitting still, though she knew he was moving at nearly twenty thousand miles an hour. She knew that because Max had just told her. See? She'd been paying attention. In two nights, he would be making his closest pass to the planet. That was the night fifteen-year-olds all over town who had been born the last time the comet came around would be making wishes for something they hoped to happen when they were thirty.

Marcy closed her eyes and focused hard on the wish she had made at fifteen, hoping Bob was listening. It was another reason she'd needed desperately to get back to Endicott this month—so that the comet would make her wish come true. There was still enough of the adolescent in her to believe wishes came true, and still enough of her fifteen-year-old self to fear that it wouldn't if she wasn't in Endicott when Bob visited. When she opened her eyes again, she wasn't sure, but she thought the comet twinkled just a little bit brighter. Maybe he had heard her. Maybe he really did understand how very important it was that he fulfill her wish.

"So tell me about these books you write."

Max's voice, still quiet and calming, washed over her from the other side of the blanket. But his question made her feel anything but quiet or calm. When she looked over at him, she saw that he had turned onto his side, his elbow planted on the ground and his head propped in his hand. He really hadn't changed at all, she thought. Even though he had changed so much. He was more handsome now than he'd been as a teenager. More self-assured. Less gawky. As if he was just more comfortable in his own skin now than he'd been back then. Marcy wished she could say the same. In a way, she did feel as if she'd gone back in time tonight. But not in a good way. Because she was starting to feel pretty gawky and in no way confident the more time she spent with Max.

Used to write, she mentally corrected him. The books she used to write. At this point, she was honestly beginning to think she would never be able to write a book again. *Seriously, Bob, I really need for you to make that wish come true. Tomorrow would be a good time. Or even the next day. But soon, okay?*

"They were… I mean, they are," she hastily corrected herself, "mysteries set in the nineteen twenties. My protagonist is named Daisy Cargill, and she's an expat American wine heiress and flapper, living in her French father's vineyard in the Loire Valley." She smiled. "She solves a lot of mysteries in the world of wine, often with her best friend, Simone, and her boyfriend, Armand. The end."

Max smiled back. "Sounds kind of Agatha Christie-ish."

"That's because they are very Agatha Christie-ish," she told him.

Belatedly, she remembered that one of the things she and Max had bonded over in science class during freshman year was the discovery that they both loved Agatha Christie novels. Judging by the way he smiled at her just then, he remembered that, too.

"I'm sorry—I haven't read any of them. Like I said, I didn't even know you were writing."

"Yeah, I kinda got that at the bookstore the other day when you asked me what I'd been doing for the last fifteen years."

He squeezed his eyes shut tight at that. "I must've sounded like a complete idiot. I am so sorry. I just don't read mysteries anymore."

"No," she replied quickly. "It was actually nice to realize I was still just Marcy Hanlon to someone for a change."

He opened his eyes again, meeting her gaze levelly. "You were never *just* Marcy Hanlon," he told her.

Something warm and fizzy blossomed in her midsection. She told it to stop doing that right now. She couldn't afford to be warm and fizzy around the man she was determined to expose as a thief.

Even so, she said, "Thanks." And she tried not to think about how warm and fizzy she sounded when she said it.

"I'll head back to Barton's tomorrow and buy the latest one," he told her.

Which meant he'd find it on the remainder table

for a fraction of its original cost and know that her writing life was as wrecked as her personal life, she realized.

"No!" she told him with a lot more force than she intended.

He must have thought so, too, because he looked at her with surprise.

"I mean…no," she said more softly. "Start with the first one. There's a developing secondary story between Daisy and Armand that I like to think plays out well when you read the books in order."

Her early books, at least, were still shelved in the regular mystery section. For now, anyway. She just hoped they were still in stock. Because they might not be, now that she thought about it.

"You know what?" she said, forcing a lightness into her voice she was nowhere close to feeling. "Just get it at the library. Save your money for a rainy day."

And, wow, if that platitude didn't make her sound like an absolutely washed-up writer, nothing did.

"Okay," he said, his tone indicating he was still a little confused by her vehement response to his offer to buy her books new. "What's the title of the first one?"

"*The Secret of the Silent Sommelier*," she told

him. Though, now that she was a more seasoned writer, she really didn't care for the titles of her first books. Nor the fact that she had been the one to title them, and her publisher had decided they had a certain distinction that might make a reader think of, well, Agatha Christie.

She continued, "It's about—"

"A silent sommelier with a secret?" Max interjected with a smile.

Marcy smiled back. "Wow, you're good."

"I have my moments."

Yes, he did. She wished he would stop it.

He looked at the remnants of their picnic, still scattered between them on the blanket. "Want another glass of wine?" he asked. "I can't drive home with it. Open container law and all that."

She knew she shouldn't. The one glass they'd shared an hour ago had been just enough to level off her anxiety about spending time with him tonight. If she had another one, it might make her feel things she shouldn't be feeling around him. Like mellow. And pleasant. And...other things she needed to fend off even more than anxiety.

Which was why it surprised her when she replied, "Sure. Why not?"

She silenced every reply her brain screamed at her in response to that and held up her glass for Max to fill. They both sat up and chatted some more about old times until the wine in their glasses was gone. Then Marcy helped him pack up what was left of their picnic and fold up the blanket. She'd walked to the park earlier, because it had been such a nice night and early enough in the evening that there were still plenty of people around. Now, though, it was after eleven, which meant the town of Endicott, even during the comet festival, would be pretty much deserted.

As if reading her mind, Max said, "C'mon. I'll give you a ride home."

He didn't seem to notice how badly he'd misspoken. What he was thinking was her home wasn't her home at all. Not anymore. She didn't have a home right now. Not anywhere. And if Bob didn't hurry up and grant her wish, she might never have a home again.

She told Max none of that, though. She only thanked him and followed him to his car. Which was actually a battered old pickup truck. Certainly, it was perfectly appropriate for his job. But it wasn't much in keeping with the money-hungry thief she knew him to be. Maybe his other car was a Ferrari. Yeah, that must be it. He was hiding his sports car in his garage while she was there to keep her from suspecting.

But as Max closed the truck's passenger-side door behind her—with a solid *cre-e-eak* that punctuated its relic status—she couldn't help thinking he wasn't the Ferrari type. He didn't seem like the thief type, either. But he was. Even if nothing her parents had told Marcy about him had sounded like the Max she knew.

They had video, she reminded herself, even if they hadn't considered it enough to take to the police about their suspicions. She'd watched with her own eyes how Max had prowled around their house on both the first and second floors. Now, though, Marcy was beginning to wonder if he'd been in the house for a different reason. Maybe he'd just wanted to see what it looked like inside. The place was pretty legendary in Endicott. Lots of townspeople had probably wanted to see what it looked like on the inside back then. Maybe Max had just taken advantage of an opportunity to assuage his curiosity, the same way a lot of other people probably would. She just couldn't jibe the Max of the last couple of days—or of her adolescence—with the thief of her parents' allegations.

Just who the hell was Max Travers, really? she wondered. And how was she going to find out, one way or the other?

As Max pulled to a stop in front of her house—

her former house, she hastily corrected herself—
she couldn't help thinking about the two of them
as teenagers again, and how, if they ever *had* dated
back then, something like this would have been a
regular occurrence. He would have dropped her off
after a night at the movies or the diner or a host of
other possibilities, then leaned across the seat and
kissed her good-night. Her heart actually kicked
up its pace at just the thought of something like
that. Which was ridiculous, because they'd never
gone to the movies or the diner or whatever, Max
had never driven her home afterward and they'd
never shared a kiss good-night…even if, maybe,
possibly, perhaps she had thought about that very
thing a time or two when they were kids. So it
wasn't going to happen tonight, either. No matter
how often she might have thought about that on
the drive home tonight, too.

She started to reach for the passenger-side door
handle, but Max was already opening his door to
get out. "Yours won't open from the inside," he told
her. "I need to open it for you."

She wondered why he hadn't bought a new truck
when he so clearly needed one. Unless it was because he'd completely blown through her parents'
money by now. Or—maybe, possibly, perhaps—
he'd never stolen it at all.

She watched him circle the front of the car, illuminated by the headlights, until he arrived at her side and opened the door for her, again with the loud creak. They both chuckled at the sound as she climbed out, then laughed harder when it groaned again as he closed it.

"You need a new truck," she said when she was standing beside him.

"Nah, this one's fine," he replied. "There's usually never anyone in the front seat with me." His gaze met hers, and something in her midsection caught fire. "Well. Not until tonight," he added.

She decided not to dwell on the significance of that statement. Instead, she told him, "Thanks for the lift." And she hoped she didn't sound as breathless as she felt when she said it.

"No problem."

They stood looking at each other in silence for a moment. Marcy had no idea what to do. A voice in her head told her to stop pussyfooting around and just ask Max flat out whether or not he had done what her parents had accused him of. But another voice cautioned her to keep up the charade until she had ironclad evidence against him. What that evidence might be at this point, she had no idea. But there must be something. Maybe he still had the safe in his possession, and if she found it, that would be proof enough. Maybe, if the two of them kept talking about old times, he'd let something slip that would be self-incriminating. Maybe he would let the nice-guy facade fall long enough for her to see that there really was some kind of monster lurking beneath.

She bit back a frustrated sigh. And maybe someday the Blue Fairy would fly through her open window and turn her into a real boy.

She was about to say something—even if it would probably be something as banal as her writing these days—when Max dipped his head and began to lean forward. For one wild moment, she thought he was going to kiss her. Then, for an even wilder moment, she realized he was. He hesitated a moment before completing the action, though, as if he was giving her a chance to move away or stop him. Marcy wondered why she did neither. She wondered even more why she, in fact, tilted her own head back a little, as if in invitation. But instead of covering her mouth with his, Max only brushed his lips across her cheek and pulled back. Although his dark skin didn't betray him, she knew somehow that he was blushing. Then again, so was she.

"I, um," she stammered. "I, uh… That is… I mean… Thanks for the lift," she finally said. Then she remembered she'd already said that. So she added, "I had fun tonight."

He grinned. And there was something a little self-satisfied about the look on his face. Not smug exactly, just… No, smug, she assured herself. Mostly because she needed to keep reminding herself he couldn't possibly be as good and as decent as she remembered and as he still seemed to be.

"Hey, what are you doing tomorrow night?" he asked. He seemed immediately surprised that he had spoken the question aloud and instantly back-pedaled. "I mean, if you're free, uh… Maybe I could cook you dinner? At my place? Show you that vegetarian can actually be something other than bland?"

His place, she thought. Where he might still have her parents' safe. Sitting right out in the open with its ill-gotten wealth—whatever was left of it—spilling out where she could take a photo of it to send to the police. Hey, it could happen.

"I actually don't have any plans at all tomorrow," she told him. *Other than beating myself up again over the fact that I won't be able to write a single coherent word.* "I'd like that."

The part about dinner, she meant. Not the part about her inability to write even a halfway decent sentence.

He smiled. "Great. I can pick you up here? Around, say, six?"

She smiled, too. Though, she realized, it wasn't entirely because of the potential opportunity to right the wrong of her parents' theft. "Sounds perfect," she told him.

And with any luck at all, it would be. Perfect for what, however, she still couldn't quite decide.

Chapter Six

Max lay awake for a long time after taking Marcy home. Normally, he fell into bed at night, exhausted from the day's labors, and was asleep pretty much the minute his head hit the pillow. But today had just been so bizarre, running the gamut from the dreadful to the divine, from the apprehension of searching for Finn Foley to the exhilaration of kissing Marcy Hanlon. Even if it had only been on the cheek, it had been their first kiss. And it had been everything he could have ever dreamed. It had been perfect. The whole night had been perfect. The sky was perfect. The breeze was perfect. The wine was perfect.

Marcy was perfect.

She'd been perfect since third grade. Doubtless she'd been perfect since birth, but third grade was when the Marcy clock had started running for Max. That clock hadn't always kept the best time. It had almost always run slow or fast, and occasionally had stopped. Tonight, though, that clock had run exactly the way it was supposed to. Tonight, that clock had been perfect, too.

He rolled onto his back and stared at the ceiling fan turning laconically overhead. What he saw, though, at least in his mind's eye, was Marcy as she sat beside him on the blanket at the park, her eyes the same clear blue as the flowers on her dress. Even after the park lights had gone out, and she was bathed only in moonlight, her eyes had shone brighter than the stars overhead. He didn't think he would ever grow tired of looking into Marcy's eyes.

He wondered where she would go when she left Endicott after this week.

That thought, too, was keeping him awake. She'd said something in the garden that morning about how she didn't want anyone in town to know about her failed marriage, at least until after she left. At the time, Max hadn't really had a chance to think about it. Now he did. She hadn't said where she was living now, or even what place she'd left to come here for the festival. It was clear she was living stateside now that her marriage was over, but what state? New York, where she'd lived in college before she got married? San Francisco, where she'd lived before that? Or was she some-place closer to home?

No matter where it was, she'd be returning to it in a matter of days. They'd made plans to attend Mrs. Barclay's gala together Friday night. That was the official end of the comet festival, even if there would be hangers-on around town for an-other week. She'd said her reservation at the inn was through Sunday morning, though, so there was still the opportunity to see her for a couple of days beyond the gala. But what happened Sunday after-noon? Would she find a way to extend her stay, or would she be all packed and ready to leave, never to return again?

It bothered Max a lot that, in spite of all the time they'd spent together over the past few days—and in spite of all the googling he'd done about her—he still knew so little about who Marcy was now. Tomorrow night, he told himself. He'd ask her all about everything tomorrow night. Tonight, he then reminded himself, since it was after midnight. The realization made him smile. Tonight, he promised himself, would be as perfect as the evening he'd just enjoyed. Because tonight, Marcy would be with him here at his house. And that…

Well, that was just perfect.

Those words echoed in his ears that evening when he went to pick her up at her house. The house that wasn't hers anymore and hadn't been for a long time. The house he'd been forbidden to enter when he was a teenager. The house he could go into now whenever he wanted, invitation or no. The house that had been purchased with his tax dollars so, in a way, he was an owner now. He'd never thought about it like that before. That Marcy's house, having been purchased, at least in part, by taxes he paid to the city and state, belonged to everyone in that city and state, including him. But not her. It was a weird realization.

It hadn't always been that way, of course. Although Mr. and Mrs. Hanlon hadn't had a problem with his employer, Mr. Bartok, coming into the house to use their bathroom or grab a glass of water or whatever, they'd made clear that wasn't the case for Max. In spite of that, he had actually been in the house when he worked there before— once. It was an event that had ended, well, badly. It had been an unseasonably hot spring day not long before the Hanlons moved, and he'd drunk all the water in his water bottle, right down to the melted ice. Since the water from the hose was warm and gross-tasting—not to mention possibly noxious—he'd decided to go to the back door and ask Mrs. Hanlon point-blank if he could come in and use the kitchen faucet. When no one responded to his knock, Max had done what any thirsty teenager would have done. He arrogantly decided he had the same right to clean fresh water that his employer did and, as he had seen Mr. Bartok do on many, many occasions, he turned the knob and entered the house without explicit permission.

He could still remember the chill of the air conditioner washing over him when he did. His own family had rarely used their AC because his parents had been so frugal. The Hanlons must have kept theirs at sixty degrees, so gloriously cold was it in the kitchen that day. Boldly, Max had made his way to the sink and turned on the cold full blast. Then he filled his bottle, drained it and filled it again. And then…

He sighed now, thinking about it. Then he'd been an idiot teenager. Instead of going back out the way he'd come in, he'd decided he wanted to see how the better half lived. How the Hanlons lived. How, specifically, Marcy Hanlon lived.

He'd left the kitchen to enter the house proper, having no idea where he was going. After checking out a few rooms on the first floor—a home office, what appeared to be a music room and a spectacular library paneled in cherrywood—he'd come to a huge sweeping staircase. And he'd figured upstairs was as good a place to look for Marcy's room as any. At the end of the longest hallway he'd ever been in outside of school, he found it.

The door had been open, as it had been for every room he passed, which was the only reason he found it as easily as he did. And through that door had been an absolute wonderland, painted deep lavender and populated by more plush animals than Toys "R" Us could shake a stick at. He remembered envying Marcy's floor-to-ceiling shelves crammed with books, not to mention her own personal gaming system and TV. He'd had to share a room with both his brothers when he was a kid, and the fights over which of the three of them would be able to use the two controllers had been epic. They'd all shared one bookcase, too—one shelf each. Max hadn't been able to imagine what it must be like for Marcy, to have all that to herself.

As he'd turned to leave, his gaze lit on her dresser, where sat an open jewelry box. Sitting to one side, just under an assortment of earrings was a rhinestone hair…thing she'd left there. He remembered seeing her wear it at the holiday band recital at Christmas and how fascinated he'd been by the way it sparkled whenever she moved her head. To this day, he had no clue why he'd done what he did next. He'd just pushed the earrings aside and grabbed it without thinking, then shoved it into his pocket. By then, he'd known Marcy would be moving. And that she'd be moving soon. He supposed he'd just wanted some kind of memento to carry with him—literally—after she was gone.

After that, feeling sweaty and shaky, he'd fled. He was halfway down the first-floor hall when Mr. Hanlon's *booming* voice from behind stopped him. Max was amazed that he hadn't vomited all over the hallway runner that had probably cost more than his parents' house while Marcy's dad read him the riot act. Mr. Hanlon had threatened him with everything from jail time, to hard labor, to the back of his hand. He probably would have exiled Max to a penal colony if there had been any left. Then Mr. Hanlon had grabbed him by his shirt collar and dragged him down the rest of the hall and through the kitchen, shoving him out the back door with enough force to send Max to his knees and slammed the door behind him.

Max had figured that would be the end of his

employment with Mr. Bartok and the job tending a garden he'd loved more than almost anything in the world. Weirdly, though, Mr. Bartok had never said a word to him. He hadn't acted any differently around Max at all, had still been his usual good-natured, amiable self. Either he hadn't seen anything wrong with what Max had done—unlikely, since Mr. Bartok was a stickler for following rules—or else Mr. Hanlon never mentioned it to him. Which was also unlikely, since Marcy's dad always seemed to be looking for an excuse to come down on Max for whatever he could. Max had decided not to question it and count himself lucky. And even when he acknowledged to himself that it had been wrong to steal Marcy's hair thing from her room, he'd had no idea how to return it to her without seeming, at best, cringey and, at worst, stalkery.

He still had that rhinestone hair thing. It was in his top dresser drawer, in a basket of odds and ends he'd collected over the years and didn't know what to do with. He supposed he could confess to Marcy now what he'd done that day and return it to her. They could share a laugh about the dumb stuff teenagers did with their not quite fully developed brains. Of course, if she did end up leaving town again, that would mean he no longer had something to remember her by.

He shook off his memories as best he could and pulled out his phone. He and Marcy had exchanged numbers at the park the night before, so when he entered the former-foyer-now-lobby of the former-house-now-hotel, he texted her to let her know he was here. A few minutes later, she was striding down the stairs he himself had crept up and down fifteen years ago. She was wearing another one of those flowy dresses, this one in a color he knew many people called rose, even though he'd never seen a rose that color in nature. At the moment, he didn't care, because on Marcy, it was the most beautiful color—the most perfect color—he had ever seen.

She came to a stop on the bottom step, right in front of him, which brought her eye-to-eye with him. "Hi," she said.

"Hi," he replied. And, for the life of him, he couldn't think of a single other word to say.

Marcy didn't seem to know what to say, either, because she just stood there staring back at him, her gaze locked with his. Finally, and a little dreamily, she told him, "You have the most interesting eyes. I always thought they were a mix of gray and blue, but there's some green in there, too."

She might as well have told him he'd grown an extra nose, so surprised was he by the statement. She'd noticed his eyes that much?

"I mean, I guess it's the shirt," she added in reference to the fern-green camp shirt he'd thrown on for the occasion, still sounding a little distracted. "But they're really beautiful."

She seemed to realize how much she had revealed—not that Max minded at all—because she suddenly snapped out of her reflection and back to the here and now.

"Sorry," she quickly said. "Didn't mean to get all mushy."

"It's fine," he assured her. "I don't mind. I got my dad's eyes. Mom and Lilah both have brown eyes, and Zach and Gabe have a mix of brown and green. Genetics are weird."

And they were. The Travers kids all had different skin tones, too, even coming from the same parents. And different hair colors and types. His parents really couldn't have been more different, physically speaking. His dad's ancestry was tied exclusively to the British Isles, and his mom's family still resided in Ethiopia, where they'd been living as far back as any of them could remember. She was dark brown, his dad was lily white and their kids were everything in between.

"Genetics *are* weird," she agreed. "All four of us Hanlon kids came from the same parents, but we couldn't be more different from each other."

Well, Max didn't know about that. Certainly, Marcy was different from the rest of them. And her mother, probably, in some ways—Max had always gotten the impression that Mrs. Hanlon was no happier to be married to her husband than Max was to work for him. But her brothers were all cut from the same cloth as far as Max was concerned, even if they didn't much physically resemble each other outside of their builds. And it was the same pinstriped cashmere that epitomized their father.

"All set?" he asked in an effort to change a subject that very much needed changing.

"All set," she assured him.

Marcy smiled as Max crooked his elbow, then slid her arm through his. She hoped he couldn't hear her heart pounding in his ears the way she did as they made their way out to his truck. The sun hung low in the sky, burnishing everything in soft golds and ambers. The wind kicked up softly and blew a strand of her hair over her eyes, and they both reached for it at the same time. Max got there first, though, and gently guided the strand back, tucking it behind her ear. It was an innocent touch that should have barely registered. Somehow, though, it made something inside her that was already wound too tautly cinch tighter still.

He opened the creaky door and helped her inside, then made his way around the front to the driver's side. She remembered him telling her no one ever rode on this side of the seat, something that suggested he didn't date much. Or at least hadn't for a while. Until tonight. This was a date, right? Unless maybe he had only invited her to dinner as a friend and was just being polite for old times' sake? When he kissed her last night, it had just been a chaste little peck on the cheek, and she had been surprisingly disappointed by that. Maybe she was wrong, thinking there had been something else going on between them over the past few days besides reigniting an old friendship that had never really been that much of a friendship. Maybe he still just wanted to be friends. Maybe she'd been completely misreading him this week.

And why did it bother her so much that that might be the case?

"This is seriously the only vehicle you have to drive?" she asked when he was sitting behind the wheel.

"Yep," he told her. "This gets me wherever I want to go. I don't need anything else."

Meaning he wasn't concerned about impressing—or even accommodating—a potential romantic interest. So maybe he didn't see her as a romantic interest. Which, of course, was fine, because, naturally, she didn't expect—or even want—anything romantic to blossom between them. She still wasn't positive he wasn't a thief. How could she possibly want—or even expect—something romantic to blossom between them?

Max made his way down the road that used to be her driveway and headed toward town. His farm, she knew, was on the other side of Endicott, meaning she would get to see many of her old proving grounds as they drove. She hadn't really done much sightseeing since her return. She hadn't even gone into town for any length of time since that first day, when she saw Max at the bookstore. Part of the reason for her self-isolation was her hope that she might get some writing done while she was here—*hah*—and part was due to her wanting to just keep a low profile and avoid seeing people she would have to talk to or, worse, reminisce with.

As she and Max drove through Endicott proper now, though, she smiled at the places she recalled from her childhood and adolescence. Not just the shops she'd loved, but the mailbox where she used to secretly mail fan letters to the Jonas Brothers every week. And there were the bushes dividing the Mazzoni and Patel houses behind which she'd received her first kiss—from Rajiv Patel when she was twelve. And there was the elm tree at the entrance to Amanda's old neighborhood, where Marcy and her friends would ditch their bikes in a pile, then sit and talk about which boys were cutest or which girls wore the coolest clothes. Really, she should make an effort to look up her old friends before she left. It actually might be kind of nice to hear what they were up to, even if she did have to come clean about her own disastrous, post-Endicott life.

"What are you thinking about?"

As always happened when she was losing herself in her memories—which had happened a lot since her return—Max's voice seemed to be coming from a long time ago and a galaxy far, far away.

She smiled. "I was just thinking about when I lived here before and all the stuff I used to do with Amanda and Claire when we were kids."

"Have you seen them much since you left town?" he asked.

She hadn't even looked them up to see if they still lived here. She hadn't spoken to either of them for more than a decade. They'd stayed friends on social media after Marcy moved, and they'd talked on the phone from time to time, but she'd deleted all of her accounts in college upon learning about her father's indictment and severed ties with virtually everyone she'd ever known. She hadn't been able to bear the questions she knew her friends would ask about him once the news was made public. Not that the news was ever widely known, thanks to Remy's efforts. Marcy still hadn't wanted to take any chances.

"I haven't," she told Max. "I wasn't even sure they still lived here."

"Amanda does," he said. "She's married with two kids and lives up the street from her parents. Claire got a full ride to Michigan State for field hockey and then moved to, I think, Grand Rapids. Last I heard, she and her partner own a couple of cannabis dispensaries. But she's back for the festival. You should look them both up."

Max might as well have told her Amanda was raising the dead in her basement, and Claire was living her life as a manatee. Amanda had always sworn she would be single for the rest of her life so that she could circle the globe as many times as possible, and Claire had been so uptight about chemical or herbal enhancements when they were teenagers, she wouldn't even take ibuprofen. She was definitely going to have to reconnect with them both somehow.

Before she could comment on either of her friends, though, Max was talking again.

"So what will you do after you check out of the inn Sunday?"

She was kind of surprised he hadn't asked the question before now. Not that she would have been prepared for it at any point. She couldn't afford to stay any longer than she was. It had been all she could do to scratch up enough money for even that.

"I don't have plans to stay in Endicott," she told him, deliberately being vague. At least it was the truth.

When she didn't clarify, she sensed, more than saw, him glance over at her, but she kept her gaze on the passing scenery. She pretended she was too wrapped up in it to notice his attention. Thankfully, he was a dutiful driver and returned his attention to the road after a second or two.

"So you're leaving?" he asked.

She truly didn't know. Part of her couldn't wait to get out of town. But another part of her—a bigger part—wished she could stay forever. How she could manage that, though, was beyond her. If Bob would just get off his duff and grant her wish...

All she said to Max, though, was "I'm not sure yet."

She did look at him then, but he had his gaze fixed firmly on the road ahead. The wind bustled through his open window, tousling his curls and blowing them over his forehead. They were moving away from the town and its immediate environs now. The Lambert farm—Max's farm, she corrected herself, the one he may or may not have bought with her parents' money—wasn't too much farther down the road. Only a few more minutes until they arrived. But there was enough time for Max to ask her questions she'd really prefer not to answer.

"So what place do you call home these days, anyway?"

Like that one.

She had no idea how to answer it. She didn't really call anyplace home these days. Even when she'd been living in a fixed place, deep down, that place had never felt truly like home. Not the way Endicott had. Not the way Endicott still did, she made herself admit. The moment she'd arrived in town last weekend, she'd felt as if she was breathing genuine air for the first time in fifteen years. Most recently, though, she'd lived in New York. So she decided that was probably the closest thing she had to, at least, a residence. Even though the residence she'd left before coming home had belonged to someone else. Before coming to Endicott, she hastily corrected herself.

"I was in New York before I came here," she said, congratulating herself for being able to tell the truth again.

"New York City?" he asked.

She nodded, then, when she realized he was still focused on driving, she clarified, "Manhattan."

"You have a place there?"

"I did," she replied before she could stop herself. Though that was true, too. She'd just had a place there years ago, that was all.

Now he glanced at her quickly before returning his gaze to the road. "But you don't anymore?"

"I didn't renew the lease on my apartment," she told him. The one she'd moved out of when she married Ollie and moved to France. Let him think of that what he would.

What he thought, however, she had no idea. Because he said nothing more about it. On one hand, she was grateful. It was a subject she really didn't want to think about right now. On the other hand, she knew she had to make plans quickly. In a matter of days, she'd be roomless in addition to being homeless.

Thankfully, the entrance to Max's farm appeared on the right. When the Lambert family lived there, there had been a big, hand-painted sign advertising produce for sale, with little hooks to hang smaller signs, depending on what was in season. She remembered that, in the summer, when she visited with her mother for peaches, there would be seemingly dozens of little signs for berries and cherries and corn and tomatoes and everything else that grew during those months. In the fall, when they came for apples, it would be things like squash and pears and pumpkins and carrots. The Lamberts had grown all kinds of things, and Marcy had never understood why her mother didn't buy more. Now, of course, she knew it was because her mother had never cooked—their housekeeper had. She'd just liked fresh peaches and apples for her own snacking. The sign, Marcy saw now, was still there and still hand-painted. But it stated only, Peaches in summer. Apples in fall. Help yourselves.

Since the truck was slowing, Marcy rolled down her window as they drove toward the house, inhaling the sweet aroma of the apple orchard in all its full, ripening glory. There was a family in there right now, taking Max at his word. Their SUV was parked with its tailgate open, and two small kids, whose ages Marcy couldn't possibly have guessed because she knew nothing of children, were dancing around it as their mother loaded a canvas bag of fruit inside. A third child, of indeterminate gender and smaller than the others, was in the father's arms. He was lifting the child up to one of the trees, and the child squealed with delight as they tugged an apple free.

Max slowed his truck as he and Marcy drew nearer, stopping when he was alongside them.

"Hey there, Lynette and Jack," he said to the parents.

He quickly introduced Marcy, who greeted them in return, then he looked at the little boys crawling in and out of their vehicle.

"Holy crow, is that you, Colin?" he said to one of them.

The bigger of the boys nodded shyly from behind his mother's legs.

"How did you get so big?" he asked. "And you, too, Dylan," he said to the other boy. "I swear you both double in size every time I see you."

The little boys laughed, but neither said a word.

"It's from eating your apples and peaches," his mother replied, laughing. "Sally is finally old enough to eat them, too, now."

Jack, the father, joined the rest of his family then, the little girl in his arms—still in diapers by the look of it—gnawing on the apple she'd just picked. Marcy would have been concerned about pesticides, but knowing what she did of Max, it was a safe bet he didn't use them. He'd said he was letting the place return to its natural state.

"Whoa, look at you, Sally," he said to the little girl. "You've got a whole mouth full of teeth now."

She tucked her head bashfully into her father's neck. But she smiled at Max with clear adoration.

"Thanks again, Max, for doing this," Lynette said. "We really love coming out here with the kids. If they had their way, we'd be here every day."

"Come anytime you want," he told them. "There's plenty. And next time, Jack, bring your folks. I'd love to see them again."

"Will do!" he promised as he corralled his family and got them loaded into the SUV.

Max waved as the family drove away, and Marcy marveled at the exchange he'd just had with them. How was he so easygoing with everyone? she wondered. Even with people she knew well, she had never been able to completely let down her guard. But Max had spoken to those kids as if they were his own. And even if they hadn't had much to say in return, they obviously liked him a lot.

"Hey, I want to pick some apples, too," she said impulsively. She had no idea what possessed her to make the statement. It had just been so sweet, watching the family picking theirs, Mom and Dad so cheerful, their children all pink-cheeked and adorable, all of them so wholesome and affectionate and happy to be together. Families like that were so alien to her. She'd never shared the kind of experiences with her own family that they must take for granted. Just once, she wanted to see what it was like to do something so simple and charming and old-fashioned. Whenever she'd come to the farm with her mother, the apples had already been bagged up for sale.

Max looked at her, surprised. "Really?"

She nodded.

"You're not exactly dressed for it."

"There are a lot of apples on low branches," she pointed out. "We don't have to use a ladder or anything. And it would be nice to have something to take ho— I mean…back to the inn," she quickly corrected herself. "For snacking."

He continued to look at her as if he wasn't quite sure what to make of her. "Okay," he relented. "Pretty sure there's a basket in the back of the truck we can use."

He switched off the engine and climbed out, coming around to Marcy's side to open her door. Sure enough, there was an old wicker basket in the truck bed that he plucked out for them to use. Thankfully, she had worn flat sandals, so the grassy terrain was easy to navigate. As they drew nearer the orchard, the scent of the apples grew stronger, surrounding her with their fresh, plummy aroma. At first, she didn't pick anything, so content was she to just be amid the trees, enjoying their fragrance. As they walked, though, one would catch her eye because of its color or shape, and she would pluck it free to put into the basket.

As they walked, Max talked to her about how, even with him rewilding the place, the trees still produced plenty of fruit on their own, thanks to, literally, the birds and the bees. But he didn't stop there; he went into explicit detail—well, explicit when it came to plant biology—about how some plants fertilize themselves, what with stamens and stigmas and pollen tubes that enter the ovule to deliver the nuclei. Except that the way he spoke, a little softer and huskier and more bewitchingly than usual, it was way too easy for Marcy to replace people parts with plant parts, and then the images just started getting way too graphic for her to let him finish describing whatever it was that passed for a plant orgasm, since she was way too close to a person one herself. But when she looked at him, he'd already stopped talking, and she could tell that he had started thinking the same way she was thinking, and he was regretting it as much as she was, except not really, because there was a part of him, like there was a part of her, that was wondering what it would be like for their own stamens and stigmas and pollen tubes, and then—

"Okay, I think I'm good," she said—a little too breathlessly—battling another wave of, um, pollination. "And I'm getting hungry," she added, hoping like hell after the fact that she had sounded hungry for food and not, you know, pollination.

Thankfully, Max pretended not to notice. He only took the basket from her hand and wove her fingers through his, ostensibly to keep her from tripping over the uneven earth, even though she'd managed just fine up until now on her own. As their fingers curled together, a current of heat sparked in her hand and rushed up her arm, pooling in her chest, where it hummed happily. When she braved another look at him, she saw that his eyes were dark and his lips were parted, as if he was having as much trouble catching his breath as she was.

It was going to be an interesting night.

They set the basket of apples in the truck for her to take to the inn later, then made their way to the house. Max was still holding her hand when they climbed the porch steps and didn't release it when he pulled his keys out of his pocket with his free hand to unlock the door. The house that had seemed so rickety and dull when Marcy was a girl looked fresh and new now. The dingy white clapboard had been painted barn-red, and the crumbling concrete stoop leading to the front door had been replaced by a covered wooden porch that spanned the entire front of the house. It was dotted here and there with hanging baskets of greenery, and it had a wicker swing swaying at one end and a pair of matching chairs and table sitting at the other.

She would never have guessed a single man lived here. It just looked too comfortable and cozy. It was the perfect place to raise a family, she thought. And now that she did think about it, she was honestly kind of surprised Max hadn't already married and started one. Any woman would have been ridiculous to turn him down. And he'd been so great with the children earlier. He'd be a wonderful husband and father.

"The house looks amazing," she told him. And then, because she couldn't quite help herself, she added, "It must have cost a fortune to do all the renovations."

"I did most of it myself," he said.

Which was a lot of trouble to go to if he could have just written a check with a stolen fortune and have someone else do it instead. The more time

Marcy spent with Max, the more she began to think her parents were wrong about him. She just didn't see how he could be so sweet and kind and hard-working and still be a villain. Then again, probably a lot of villains could be sweet when they wanted to be. Even Blofeld in the James Bond movies loved his cat while being a criminal mastermind trying to take over the world. Maybe Max's decency was genuine. Maybe he'd had his reasons for doing what he did fifteen years ago.

Or maybe, she thought, he just didn't do it. Maybe the video of him roaming around in their house really had been about something else. From what she'd learned and seen of Max since she'd been back, she just didn't see how it was possible that he could be someone who would do the wrong thing. Who would betray a trust placed in him. Who would commit a crime. And if he *had* committed a crime as a teenager, he seemed like the kind of man who would own up to it and try to make things right. She simply was not as sure of his guilt now as she had been before she returned to Endicott. In fact, she was becoming more sure with every passing minute that he was almost certainly innocent. Her parents had clearly made a mistake.

Clearly.

But if it hadn't been him, what was she going to

do now? She'd made a wish on Bob fifteen years ago, one she fiercely needed to come true. If Max wasn't the one who had ruined her family's life— and ruined her life, too, by extension—then who had? And how was she going to find that person and make them pay and return things to the way they'd been?

She shook off the thoughts, since they were even more troubling than the ones she'd had of Max's apparent guilt. Instead, she looked at his charming house again. Sitting on this porch in the evenings while owls hooted and fireflies twinkled must be a glorious pastime. She could spend a lot of time on this porch doing exactly that. She looked at Max again. Maybe…

She shook off that thought, too, before it could dare materialize. "I can't believe you did all this by yourself," she told him.

"Well, I had help from Felix and Chance, and my family when they were able to. I did most of the work inside, too," he added proudly. "Left the wiring and plumbing to the professionals, of course, but the rest of it…pretty much all yours truly."

As if to illustrate that, he pushed open the front door and held the screen door, gesturing for her to precede him. "Come on in," he told her with a smile. "Dinner will be ready soon."

Chapter Seven

Max held his breath as Marcy moved past him and into his house. He really had put a lot of work into the place. When he bought it three years ago, he'd thought it would be a great spot to raise a family, even though starting a family hadn't even been on his radar at that point. It still wasn't. He'd only ever been able to picture having a family with Marcy, but he'd never had a clue how things between them would turn out. He wasn't even sure where things were going right now. In spite of the weird…chemistry that had passed between them when he was describing pollination to her—and what the hell had possessed him to even do that?—

he still wasn't sure what, exactly, was what. Were they still old acquaintances? Were they friends? Were they each gauging the other to see if there was the potential for something else? Something that maybe had been germinated when they were teenagers but never had the chance to blossom? Or was it something entirely new happening for the first time between them because they were adults?

There had been times this week when he'd thought the two of them were enjoying something that bordered on romance. But there had been other times when he'd sensed a distance in Marcy that was unmistakable. Times when she seemed to like him a lot and times when she seemed a little chilly. Her signals were mixed. So were his feelings. Maybe tonight, having her here in his space without the distractions of the outside world, would give them both a chance to figure things out.

Sodo sauntered down the stairs to greet them, then sat back on her haunches in front of Marcy to smile her goofy doggy smile.

"This is Sodo," Max said. Then he turned to the dog. "Sodo, this is Marcy. Be nice."

"Oh, I bet Sodo is always nice," she said. He smiled when he noted she was speaking in the tone of voice people used when meeting someone else's pet for the first time. "Who's a good boy? Or girl?"

"Girl," Max said. "And, yeah, she is definitely a good one."

Marcy bent to scritch behind the dog's ear. "How did she get the name *Sodo*?"

"She's named after the town where my mom grew up in Ethiopia."

The dog turned her head into the ear rubbing, and Marcy smiled again. When she finally stopped and straightened, Sodo looked devastated. But she ambled off to her doggy bed beneath the front window and curled herself into it. Max held his breath as Marcy surveyed her surroundings. Where the living room used to be tiny and crowded with peeling wallpaper and a shag carpet, it was now a wide-open space of creamy walls and polished hardwood. His furnishings were simple but classic, secondhand midcentury modern pieces he'd refinished himself and framed prints of all things botanical. He'd striven for tranquility when he put the room together, and he liked to unwind here when he came home at the end of the day. Even now, all the tension that had been wrapping him since leaving to pick up Marcy slowly began to ease. He hoped she was feeling less nervous about the evening, too.

"This is a really wonderful room," she said. "I could spend a lot of time in this room."

The words flowed over him like a warm embrace.

He'd like it very much if she would spend a lot of time here. Like, maybe, the rest of her life.

"It's beautiful, Max," she continued, her admiration clear in her tone. "I can't believe how different it is from when the Lamberts lived here."

He smiled. "Thanks. It's been a labor for sure, but a labor of love. There's still a lot to do upstairs. I'm only done with my office up there. But this floor is pretty much where I want it to be. My bedroom's through there—" he nodded to their right "—and the kitchen and dining room are this way."

He tugged on her hand and led her in that direction. The kitchen and dining room had been separate rooms before, but he'd knocked out a wall to turn it into one big one that spanned the back of the house. The space was minimalist but, he hoped, as welcoming as the living room, its maple four-seat table currently decorated with a simple centerpiece of—he hadn't been able to help himself—lobelias and dogwood blossoms. Wineglasses gleamed in the early evening sun slanting through the wide windows that filled both walls in that corner. They were more new additions that showcased the brilliant view the room boasted of the rolling green hills and massive expanse of now-sunset-streaked sky.

He normally didn't spend a lot of time in the

kitchen, but, like everything else when he'd redone the place, he'd wanted the room to be inviting and relaxing. The appliances weren't state-of-the-art, but they weren't low-budget. The three big pots sitting atop the stove weren't state-of-the-art, either, but they all came from a matching set. The walls were pale blue, the countertops gray-and-cream granite. The one by the sink was heaped with fresh produce in preparation for the not-bland dinner he would make for Marcy tonight—onions, garlic, tomatoes, bell peppers. Not to mention red lentils, fresh ginger and a host of spices.

As she looked around, Max went to work on dinner preparations. When he glanced up, though, what she really seemed to be looking at were his hands as he chopped. Or maybe his arms. Or maybe both. Anyway, whatever she was looking at, she seemed to be pretty interested. Enough that two bright spots of pink appeared on her cheeks. He was about to ask her if she was okay, when she finally shook her head slightly, as if to clear it, and looked at his face instead. Her eyes were wide and dark. "Um, what's the, uh, green stuff you're cutting?" she asked, her voice strained.

"Collard greens," he told her.

She wrinkled her nose at his reply. "Ew."

He chuckled. "They get a bad rap. If they're cooked properly, they're delicious."

"What's 'properly?'"

He held up the first spice bottle in the row, one half-filled with reddish powder. "Berbere. It's the secret ingredient in a lot of Ethiopian cooking. It's also extremely spicy, so I'll go easy on you and only use half as much as I usually do."

"No, that's okay," she told him. "I like spicy food."

He eyed her dubiously. "Famous last words of a lot of people."

"Really," she said. "One of my roommates in college was from Chengdu, and she used to make this Sichuan hot pot that was so spicy, it made us all sweat like pigs. I mean, ladylike pigs," she hastily clarified when she must have realized her simile was less than flattering. "Which I guess would make us sows," she added when she then seemed to realize her clarification hadn't helped at all. "Anyway, it was superspicy," she quickly concluded. "Cook the way you normally would. Now you've got me curious."

"Okay, if you're sure," he said, still doubtful.

"I'll sign a waiver if you want."

He smiled. "Not necessary. If you burst into flames, I'll just toss some baking soda on you."

The mention of bursting into flames made her cheeks flush even more. Something inside Max grew warm, too. He really wished he knew what the hell was going on between the two of them. It would be so helpful if he could keep from embarrassing himself tonight and not do or say something inappropriate. Like bursting into flames, for example.

Thankfully, Marcy went back to inspecting his kitchen, her gaze skittering nervously from his face to everything else—the framed prints of spices, the glass-covered cabinets filled with white dishes, the colorful array of food on the countertop.

"You know, I have to admit that vegetables are very pretty," she said. "Maybe they really can be delicious in the right hands."

And why did she say that in a way that made it sound as if she was thinking about his hands performing an entirely different activity? One that had nothing to do with cooking and everything to do with, um, a different kind of heat.

She seemed to realize that, too, because she quickly switched gears again. "Hey, is there anything I can do to help?"

"Nah," he said, finishing up with an onion and reaching for one of the peppers. "Unless maybe you want to open us a bottle of wine?"

"That I can do," she said, sounding relieved to have something to occupy herself. "If nothing else good came out of my marriage, at least I now know what wines go with what dishes. Which actually helps me not at all since I never cook."

Her admission surprised Max. Not that he was a gourmet chef, either, but it seemed like something everyone did. It got expensive eating out all the time, or even bringing home takeout. And Marcy had lived in a vineyard when she was married. Wine and cooking just seemed to go hand in hand.

She seemed to read his mind again, because she told him, "Ollie and I had a chef at the villa. Before that, my two roommates cooked in exchange for me paying for the bulk of the groceries. We had a cook when my family moved to San Francisco, too. And when we lived here..."

"Here, it was Mrs. Mazzoni," Max said.

He remembered the Hanlons' cook well. Not only had he played soccer with her son, Leo, but on the nights when Max had to work late at the Hanlons', well past the dinner hour, she would also sneak food out to him after the family finished theirs. She was a nice lady.

"There was just never any reason for me to learn how to cook," Marcy said. "God knows my mom wouldn't do it. She never cooked a day in her life, either. For vegetables, even if I don't like them, we'll need a white wine." She opened the refrigerator to see what Max had to offer. Then she looked back at him. "You do realize that your entire bottom shelf is filled with wine, yes?"

"I'm not a wino," he assured her. "I just asked Felix to recommend something for tonight, and he brought over an entire case. Every bottle is something different. There's some red, too, if you'd rather have that."

"Red is usually good with spicy food," she said, "but it's a nice night for white, I think. And if Felix recommended these, I'm sure they're all excellent."

She bent to survey the wine selections in the fridge, then plucked out a bottle. "This is a really excellent sauvignon blanc. Where's the corkscrew?"

By now, Max had finished chopping the pepper, and was moving on to the garlic. "The small drawer to your left."

She found it easily and went to work on the cork, tugging it out with expert proficiency. Then she picked up the wineglasses he'd placed on the table and filled each, setting Max's on the counter next to the piles of chopped vegetables.

"What are we having tonight?" she asked.

"I'm making a few different things we can share," he told her. "*Misir wot* with the lentils, *at-*

akilt with the cabbage, carrots and potatoes, and *gomen wot* with the collards, onion, peppers and ginger."

She nodded at the row of jars lined up on the other side of him. "And lots and lots of spices besides the berbere, it looks like," she said before inspecting them. "Cardamom, cumin, turmeric… I can safely say these are no more familiar to me than the berbere you mentioned."

"And, of course, we're having *injera*, too," he added.

"Which is?"

He pointed at a roll of what he'd been told by others unfamiliar with it looked like pie dough with holes in it. "It's everything," he said. "Plate, utensil, flatbread, delicious." Her confusion was clear in her expression, so he smiled and added, "You'll see. But I confess I cheated a little since I can never get my injera to turn out right, so I had my mom make that. Hers is always perfect."

Marcy smiled, but he could tell she had no idea what he was talking about. He appreciated the gesture nonetheless. She really did seem a lot less harried tonight than she had been other times this week. He remembered her animation when she'd impulsively told him she wanted to pick apples. She'd been as excited as a little kid. He liked that

she was enjoying herself at his place. He liked it a
lot. And he found himself hoping she stayed longer
in Endicott than Sunday morning. Because he really wanted to have her here again. Lots of agains.
Like, maybe a lifetime of agains.

"I think we're good to go," he said, halting his
thoughts before they could get away from him.
As they had been doing a lot this week. "This can
all pretty much come together at the same time."

He took a moment to enjoy a swallow of wine,
then began turning on burners on the stove. He
added olive oil to one pot, vegetable broth to another and niter kibbeh—which, he explained to
Marcy when she asked, was a spiced, clarified butter—to a third one. He kept her apprised of everything he was doing, and when it came time to add
the spicy berbere to the collards, he dropped in a
generous amount, then threw her a look that said,
You sure that's not too much?

To her credit, she did look a little concerned.
"Wow, that really is a lot of spicy spice," she said.

He gave the food a generous stir, then dipped in
a spoon and offered her a taste. He could tell by her
expression that she definitely found it *hot*. Maybe
even hotter than her old roommate's Sichuan dish.
There was every chance her roomie had tempered

her cooking to suit Western tastes, too, and had just wanted to be polite about it.

Marcy fanned her mouth theatrically after swallowing. "Okay, so I'm not bursting into flames, but much more of that, and I will be."

Max nodded sagely. "Yeah, that was a little over half the amount my mom uses."

She nodded back, less sagely. "Well, alrighty then. I stand corrected."

Once everything was done, Max rolled out the injera onto a wide round platter his mother had given him as a housewarming gift for an occasion precisely like this one. Then he piled each of the dishes he'd created in its center, so that none was quite touching any of the others.

"I'll set the table," Marcy offered when she realized the table now only held two napkins.

"Not necessary," he told her. "But we will need to wash our hands."

After doing that, he carried the platter to the table and placed it on one corner, within easy reach of both chairs there. Even the napkins weren't customary for the way Ethiopian food was generally served, he knew. But he didn't want Marcy to be *too* overwhelmed by what was to come.

"But…dishes?" she asked again.

"We don't need them," he told her. "Like I said,

the injera is everything. Well, okay, we will need the wine. You could bring that to the table."

Marcy retrieved it from the fridge and, after topping off their glasses, set it near the food. She was still obviously confused when Max pulled out her chair for her, but she seated herself dutifully. He sat, too, on the chair beside hers. She looked at the food, then at the empty place on the table in front of her, then at Max.

"I have no idea what I'm supposed to do next," she told him.

He grinned. "Ethiopian meals are generally communal," he said. "Everyone eats off the same plate. And we don't traditionally eat with utensils. We eat with our hands."

Before she could point out the obvious—that some of the food on the platter looked kind of hard to handle with fingers alone—he tore off a piece of the injera at its edge, pinched it over the dish closest to him, which happened to be the *gomen wot*, then lifted it to his mouth, popping it deftly inside.

"There. See?" he said after he swallowed. "Easy."

She eyed him suspiciously but did her best to mimic his efforts. He watched as she tore off a piece of injera he knew would be too small and aimed for the *misir wot*, grabbing way too much of it for the flatbread to hold. Sure enough, some of the lentils dribbled out over her fingers before she could get them wrapped, then those fell onto the table as she quickly moved her hand to her mouth. The good news was she didn't spill any on her dress. The bad news was her chin didn't fare so well. She quickly grabbed a napkin.

"Guess you go through a lot of these, huh?" she asked when she'd finished cleaning herself up.

"Actually, the napkins are a courtesy for you. Ethiopians don't really use them."

"So, what, you just lick your fingers?"

Max made a face at her. "Gross, no, that would be incredibly impolite. We just don't get food all over our hands. But hey, that was a good effort," he added in the same tone of voice he might have used for one of the players on the youth league soccer team he coached every spring. "Next time, try a bigger bit of injera with a little less *misir wot*."

This time, she was the one to make a face. "Thanks, Dr. Science, that never would have occurred to me."

He laughed. "Here, like this."

He repeated his initial action, this time scooping up some of the *atakilt*. Instead of guiding it to his own mouth this time, though, he moved his hand toward hers. Marcy widened her eyes in surprise when she realized he intended to feed her.

"It's another tradition to feed others at the table,"

he told her. "In fact, I should have fed you before feeding myself. Because the most honored guest at the table should always be fed first. It's a sign of admiration and...and affection."

With every word Max spoke, his heart rate doubled, his body temperature rocketed and his breathing became more erratic. And he hadn't even touched her since they'd entered the house. She just looked so beautiful sitting there, her hair radiant with amber highlights from the setting sun, her blue eyes brilliant, the pinks and lavenders of the sunset streaking the sky behind her. He didn't think he'd ever seen her looking more beautiful than she did in that moment. And he'd seen Marcy Hanlon looking pretty damn stunning in the past. She was always stunning. Always brilliant. Always radiant. Perfect. Holy crow, she was just so perfect.

Her lips parted fractionally, her own breathing none too steady. When Max moved his hand closer to her mouth, she opened it wider, and he gently tucked the bite into it without touching her or spilling a drop. Her eyes never left his as she chewed and swallowed. Though he could tell she was having a little trouble chewing and swallowing.

"Thanks," she finally said softly. "That, uh, that really is, um, good. You're right. Vegetables can be...ah, delicious. And thanks for telling me I'm the most honored guest. Then again, I'm the only guest, so…"

She smiled, but there was something a little anxious in the gesture. Max smiled, too, feeling a little anxious himself. There could have been a million guests at dinner tonight, and Marcy would still be the most honored. He was torn between feeding her again—not that he could trust himself to do it nearly as successfully this time, considering the way his head was spinning with her so close—and going back to feeding himself. She took the decision out of his hands, though, by reaching for the injera herself. This time, she had much better luck, mostly because she moved very slowly and very carefully. Maybe a little too slowly and carefully, because Max couldn't take his eyes off of her.

Even so, he tucked in again, too, and for the next few minutes, they ate in—almost—comfortable silence. But with every bite, the temperature in the room seemed to boost higher, and not because of the spiciness of the food. Every time their gazes met—and they met often—both of them seemed to realize that…something…was happening between them. An awareness that hadn't been there before. Or, if it had been, it was breaking out of its confines with the intent of making itself known in a big way. Without speaking a word, they just somehow seemed to be leaning into whatever that something was to explore it a little more closely. Finally, though, they sat back in their chairs, their meal not quite finished, each eyeing the other in silence.

As if each of them was trying to figure out what they were supposed to do next.

Marcy had been on edge ever since Max's apple-picking pollination lecture, and her entire body was still humming with the anticipation of something she couldn't—or maybe didn't want to—identify. Having him feed her the way he had at the beginning of their meal had only made it worse. Or maybe better. It depended on what she might or might not be anticipating, and since she wouldn't let herself think about what she might or might not be anticipating, it was both better and worse, which meant… Something. She wouldn't let herself think about that, either.

Now, as she sat back in her chair, twirling the last of her wine in its glass by the stem, she couldn't stop looking at him. He, too, was sipping what was left of his wine, eyeing her from over the rim of the glass in a way that made her think of dessert. Like maybe she was dessert. Or maybe he was. Again, perspective. She just wished it hadn't been so confusing lately.

"I guess we should—"

"Would you like to—"

Once again, they spoke and stopped as one. Then they each chuckled a little nervously.

"—clean up," she said, finishing her statement.

"—take our wine out to the porch to watch the sun set?" he said at the same time.

Again, they laughed. Again, they were nervous. Again, neither seemed to know what to do next.

Sitting on the porch to watch the sunset would be lovely, Marcy thought. Hadn't she just been thinking something like that a little while ago? Funnily, right now, she didn't want to do that. She didn't want to clean up, for that matter. What she really wanted was to—

"Cleanup will just take a few minutes," she pointed out. "Then we can take our wine out and enjoy the sunset."

"Good compromise," he said.

It was a good compromise, Marcy decided as they completed the first part of the plan. Funny thing, though, they never quite got to the second part. Because as she was reaching up toward a cabinet to replace a bowl, Max bent toward a drawer to replace a spoon, and his arm brushed her torso right next to her breast. Both immediately halted their actions, their gazes locking. Slowly, she replaced the bowl on the shelf and turned back to face him, an action that left his arm grazing her body even more intimately, sending a blast of heat from her breast to her heart, then to every other inch of her. Then he stepped closer to drop the spoon into the drawer beside her, sliding it shut again, an action that brought his body even closer to hers. Then he was dipping his head toward hers, and she was tipping hers back. And then…

Oh, then. Then he was kissing her with all the tenderness and softness of a summer afternoon. For long, delicious moments, he only moved his lips lightly over hers, kissing each corner of her mouth, tracing her lips with the tip of his tongue. Then he moved closer still and pulled her into his arms, covering her mouth completely with his. She opened to him willingly, fully, and when he tasted her more deeply, she curled into him with a need unlike any she had felt before. He was just so… She felt so… This whole evening was becoming so…

She curled her fingers into the front of his shirt in an effort to pull him closer, even though he was as close as he could possibly be. She wanted more of him. She needed more of him. The hands around her waist moved to her hips and pulled her closer, too—close enough that she could feel his hard length pressing against her. She uttered a wanton little sound at the realization, and he kissed her deeper still.

"Max," she whispered against his mouth. But she had no idea what she wanted to tell him.

He seemed to understand, though, because he pulled away and gazed down into her eyes, his pupils dark with want. "Do you want to stop?"

She told herself to tell him yes. She still had so many conflicting feelings about him. About herself. About everything. He made her feel so good, though. This moment felt so right. Tonight was the first time in a long time she'd felt either of those things. And even if tonight only lasted for tonight, it was more than she'd had since... Since ever.

So instead of replying with words, she pushed herself up on tiptoe, curling one hand around his nape and the other over his jaw, and kissed him again. And again. And again. Max dropped a hand to lace his fingers with hers, then, still kissing her, led her out of the kitchen. They paused a few times on the way to his bedroom to deepen their kisses and touch each other more intimately, so by the time they entered the room that was as minimalist and warm and cozy as the rest of the house, their breathing was ragged and their clothing, in disarray. They didn't stop until they were at the edge of his bed, each hesitating only long enough to take stock.

This was really going to happen, Marcy realized. She and Max were finally going to do what the two of them had been thinking about doing on some level probably since the moment their eyes met in the bookstore. Maybe even before that. When they were kids, they'd always danced shyly around an awareness of each other. Maybe even back then, in whatever way they could have as teenagers, they had been thinking about what it would be like to do this. There had been so many obstacles between them, though. Their youth, their uncertainty, social barriers, her family... Now that they were adults, there was nothing, no one, to interfere.

She suddenly felt freer than she had ever felt before. There had never been a time in her life when she didn't feel obligated to someone or something. But now she'd reached a point where she had nothing, so she had nothing to lose. Nothing except this moment with Max. There was no way she was going to let it go.

He pulled her close and kissed her again, running his hands—his deft, delicious hands—from her wrists to her shoulders and back again. Then he wove his fingers with hers again and pulled their hands between their bodies. When he kissed her more deeply, Marcy tilted her head to allow him inside her mouth, groaning at the exquisite pleasure of his entry. He released his hands from hers, and she felt them on her breasts, the backs skimming softly over her sensitive flesh before cupping them gently in each palm. She splayed her hands open over his chest, touching all the bumps of muscle that were somehow even more defined than she'd realized. Unable to help herself, she began unbuttoning his shirt. He quickly moved to help her, until the garment was lying at his feet, and then…

Oh, then. Then she saw in the mellow lamplight just how beautiful Max truly was. Her gaze went to the tattoo on his left arm, revealed for the first time, and she saw that it was a ring of delicate blue flowers winding and curling among themselves. Lobelias. Max had printed himself permanently with what he'd known was her favorite flower. She moved her fingers to the image and traced it lightly.

"Lobelias," she said softly. "You have lobelias on your arm."

"Yeah."

"Why lobelias?"

When she looked up, he was gazing down at her so fiercely, so intently, her breath caught in her throat.

"I think you know why."

"Because of me."

He nodded. "Because of you."

"Max—"

"Marcy—"

They spoke at once, then stopped at once, neither seeming ready to say whatever they had intended to say.

"You first," he told her.

She shook her head. "I don't know what to say. This isn't how I thought things were going to go when I came back to Endicott. I thought…"

"What?"

There was no way she could tell him that when she first returned, she thought he was a thief who had ruined her family. She knew now that he wasn't, and she didn't want to say anything that would make him think she hadn't had the faith in him that she should have had all along. Max had been a good kid. He was a good man. How could she have ever suspected otherwise?

"I just never thought you and I would end up this way," she finally said.

He smiled. "And I always knew that we would."

The heat flaming in her midsection spiraled outward at the absolute certainty she heard in his voice. There was nothing proprietary in it, nothing domineering. Just a knowledge he'd had all along that the two of them belonged together and that, somehow, someday, some way, they would be.

"How could you know that?" she asked. "Especially when we were kids?"

"I just did."

She gazed at the tattoo again, guiding her finger over the blossom in the middle. Her eyes never left the flower as she asked, "What were you going to say before I interrupted?"

Max hesitated, expelling a restless sigh. "I was going to tell you that I don't think I'm quite as... I mean, I'm not..." He sighed again. "Pretty sure I'm not as, um, experienced at this as you are."

Her gaze flew to his at that. "You're not... I mean you couldn't be a..."

"No," he quickly assured her. "I've...dated. I just haven't dated as many people as you seem to have dated. Not that I think you, you know, *dated*, all the guys you dated, but..." Here, he smiled a little self-consciously and uttered a self-deprecating sound. "I just haven't dated *or* dated all that much."

Clearly, once he'd discovered who she was, he'd done his internet homework on her the same way she had on him before returning to town. But where there hadn't been much about Max online other than references to his business and youth soccer coaching, she knew how many photos there were of her online that exaggerated her partying years, since that was what sold papers and garnered web site hits. She probably hadn't actually *dated* that many more people than Max had. But she could understand why he would think what he did, due to her seeming social history.

"Does that bother you?" she asked. "That I've maybe…dated…more people than you have?"

He shook his head. "No. Of course not. I just think it's important for you to know that I haven't been with that many women."

"And why is that?"

His gaze met hers again. "Because I learned pretty quickly that no other woman was you."

Her heart began racing again, and she pushed herself up on tiptoe to kiss him. Softly at first, running her lips once, twice, three times over his, then deepening them when he roped his arms around her waist and pulled her close. She felt him swell even harder against her belly, and that made her crave him even more. He found the buttons on the back of her dress and nimbly freed them one by one, then her dress was pooling at their feet. She felt his hands on her bare skin, so rough and coarse from his work, so gentle and adept from his care. So she touched him, too, everywhere she could, loving every slope and dent of muscle she encountered.

He growled something incoherent against her mouth, then moved his hands to her bra and unhooked it. It fell to the floor, just as she went to work on the button and zipper of his trousers. He dragged them off, along with the boxers beneath, then pulled her into his embrace again before she had a chance to see him bare. But she felt him, all of him, against the bare flesh of her torso. She tucked a hand between them and enclosed him, stroking her hand slowly down the length of him and back up again.

His hands went to her panties, and together they removed them. Then Max jerked down the covers of the bed and sat atop it, pulling her into his lap, facing him. He cupped the curve of her fanny in one hand as he guided the other between her legs. She cried out at the intimacy, tangling her fingers in his hair and guiding his head to her breast. As he tasted her there, he dipped a long finger inside her, removed it slowly, then eased it inside her again. His other fingers slid through the damp folds of her flesh, taking their time as they searched for that most sensitive part of her. Then—oh, oh, oh, *ooh*—he found it. Heat erupted between her legs, moving outward, until every part of her felt ready to explode.

Never, ever, ever had she experienced the kind of exhilaration she felt in that moment, giving herself over so utterly to Max. And when he lay back on the bed, pulling her atop him to kiss her again, all she could do was melt into him. For a long time, they kissed, running their hands over every part of each other they could reach, caressing, grazing, stroking. When he turned them to their sides, she moved her hand over the length of him again, palming the damp head of his shaft before dragging her fingers to its base to fondle him there. He gasped at the touch, then nipped at her lip. Then he rolled over onto his back again. In one quick, easy move, he reached into the nightstand for a condom and rolled it on. Then he pulled Marcy close again, setting her astride him so that he could enter her from below. As he grasped her hips, she leaned forward to clutch his shoulders. Then, slowly, smoothly, deeply, he pushed himself inside her.

She closed her eyes and groaned as he filled her completely. She tried to rise up to accommodate him, but he held her in place, moving deeper still. Again, she cried out, but she stilled, letting her body grow accustomed to his presence. It had been so long since she had experienced this kind of closeness with a man. No, she realized immediately. She had never experienced this kind of closeness with a man. Max fitted her perfectly. And she fitted him. It was as if their bodies had been made to come together this way, almost as if they'd been created this way at the origin of time and then separated through some cruel cosmic cataclysm, only to just now be reunited. She opened her eyes to see him gazing back at her as if he was as mesmerized by the idea as she was. Then he lifted her up over him and pulled her down again, harder this time, and she couldn't think at all.

Again and again, he moved her up and down over his shaft, the damp friction growing hotter with every stroke. Then he was turning their bodies so that she was on her side with her back to him, and, with the fingers of one hand moving between her legs and the fingers of the other caressing her nipple, he was entering her from behind. She nearly lost herself a second time until he moved them again, this time turning her onto her back beneath him, lowering himself until he could taste her breasts. Then, lower still, his head moved between her legs, his mouth wreaking such erotic chaos that she could only bend her knees to dig her heels into the mattress and tangle her fingers in the sheet to hang on. Just as she thought she would shatter into a million tiny pieces, he brought his body up again, bracing himself with a muscular forearm on each side of her head. He watched her intently as he entered her for the last time, thrusting his hips against hers, harder and harder, until they both cried out together in their completion.

And then he was beside her on his back again, pulling her close, burying his head in her neck and saying words that sounded very much like *I love you*.

She should have been terrified to hear them. She didn't want anyone to care that much for her. She wasn't sure how to handle such a powerful emotion. She'd come to realize a long time ago that she'd never been in love. Not even with Ollie. That had been infatuation and fascination and desire. It had been an attempt to escape what had become an ugly reality into what she'd hoped would be a storybook life. Marcy didn't want anyone to love her, because she couldn't love anyone herself. What she felt for Max was…complicated. She didn't know what it was. But it wasn't love. It couldn't be.

Could it?

She pretended she didn't hear him and nestled into him, too. She dragged her fingers down the sweat-slickened skin of his torso, then up again, to settle her palm over his heart. She could feel it beating against her hand, still racing as fast as her own. His still-hard shaft twitched against her, and her breath hitched quickly. He already wanted her again. She already wanted him again, too. She was beginning to think there would never come a time when she didn't want him. No one had ever made her feel the way she felt tonight.

For several long moments, they only lay together in silence. Then Max kissed her forehead and excused himself, presumably to take care of the condom. He made his way out of the bedroom, and Marcy pulled the sheet up over herself. Her skin was damp, too, and the breeze tumbling in through the open window, coupled by the laconic movement of the fan overhead, brought with it a little chill.

She heard the shower switch on somewhere beyond the bedroom door and realized Max wouldn't be returning to warm her up anytime soon. So she rose from the bed to see if she could find something of his with sleeves to do that instead. His dresser was closest, so she went to that, opening the first drawer she found. Socks. Of course. Those would be so helpful. She was about to close the drawer and move to the one below it when something twinkled in the scant lamplight, catching her eye. Twinkled like a diamond, she couldn't help thinking. It was in a small wire basket in the corner of the drawer that looked to be a catchall of sorts. She tilted her head and saw the shimmer of light again. She told herself not to snoop and just close the drawer. But something cold and unpleasant had settled in her stomach, and she knew it wasn't going to go away until she found the source of the glimmering.

Probably his high-school class ring, she thought as she slowly moved her hand toward the basket. Or maybe a newly minted dime. An ID bracelet from an old girlfriend. Or a broken geode he found outside on the ground. She moved her hand to push aside a small screwdriver and some shoelaces still in the package. Then her heart plummeted as she withdrew what it actually was.

Her great-grandmother's diamond-and-platinum hair comb. The one Marcy hadn't seen since her sophomore year of high school. The one her family normally kept in the portable safe in her father's office.

The one Max Travers, she now realized, had stolen.

Chapter Eight

Max hadn't planned to take a shower when he got out of bed, but by the time he got to the bathroom, he realized he needed one. No sense subjecting Marcy to his sweaty self for the rest of the night. He was in and out as quickly as he could be, then dried off and wrapped the towel around his waist, cinching it on one side. He had no idea how the rest of the night would play out. He knew how he hoped it would play out, in which case the towel wouldn't be necessary, either, for much longer, but that all depended on Marcy.

He still couldn't believe they'd come together the way they just had. Sure, he'd fantasized about it happening tonight—hell, he'd fantasized about it every night since she came home—but he hadn't taken anything for granted. He'd wanted to let her call the shots. And he'd been delighted when her thoughts and actions mirrored his own.

Sometimes, he thought happily, life worked exactly the way it was supposed to. Sometimes, everything just fell into place perfectly.

He padded back to his room in his bare feet to find that Marcy had risen from bed, too. She'd also gotten fully dressed, right down to her shoes, something that kind of confused him. Even if they weren't going to go back to bed, the night was young. They could sit outside with another glass of wine or, if she wasn't big on the great outdoors, they could stay in and watch a movie or something.

Maybe she wanted to go out, he told himself. Finish the evening with a drink somewhere in town. Even though that didn't seem like the kind of thing two people would want to do after the fireworks the two of them had just set off in each other. Max certainly didn't want to do it himself.

"Hey," he said quietly.

And, he had to admit, uncertainly. There was a vibe in the room that hadn't been there when he'd left it. And it wasn't exactly a good one.

"You're dressed," he added inanely when she said nothing in response.

"I'm leaving," she told him flatly.

His stomach knotted. What the hell had happened during the five minutes he was in the shower?

"Why?" he asked. "I thought we were—"

"You thought wrong," she interrupted, her voice grim.

He took a step toward her. She took one in retreat. Her expression was bleak, her eyes wet with tears. For the life of him, he could not figure out what was wrong.

"Marcy, what's going on?"

She extended her closed hand toward him, then opened her fingers. In her palm was the rhinestone hair thing he'd taken from her room fifteen years ago. Crap. He knew he should have come clean before now.

"Where did you get this?" she demanded.

He closed his eyes, hoping to stem the embarrassment that washed over him. In an effort to beat back the defensiveness assailing him, he went on the offense instead. "What were you doing going through my dresser drawers?" he asked. He knew his was the greater infraction here and that he should apologize and explain before charging her.

But he needed some time to figure out just how the hell he could apologize and explain.

She shook her head. "Oh, no. Don't you dare try to turn this around on me. My transgression is nothing compared to yours. You stole this, didn't you? Back when you worked for my family when we were kids."

There was no way he could deny it, even if he wanted to. And really, he didn't want to. He needed to tell her the truth. He didn't want there to be any secrets between him and Marcy. Things were happening faster with the two of them than he'd anticipated. Hell, things were happening with the two of them period. No way did he want to screw this up. Especially over a fifteen-year-old rhinestone hair thing.

"I did," he told her. "I'm sorry," he added when he saw the look of devastation that came over her. "It was a dumb thing to do."

He did his best to explain to her what happened that day, how the heat had been unbearable—hey, maybe he'd even had heatstroke and that contributed to his stupidity, he tried to joke—and how, once he was in her house, alone, he'd wanted to learn more about her. He told her how he'd found her room, but hadn't done more than take a quick look around, then had seen the hair thing lying in the open jewelry box on her dresser. He told her how he'd remembered her wearing it at the holiday concert a few months before and how beautiful she'd looked. And he told her how he'd just impulsively grabbed it to have a memento of her. How her dad had caught him when he was heading to go back outside and yelled at him before literally throwing him out. And he told her how sorry—oh, man, was he sorry—for what he'd taken from her room that day.

When he was finished, he waited for her to upbraid him and prepared himself for more profuse groveling and apologizing before they finally hashed it all out. Instead, tears sprang into her eyes with enough force to spill down her cheeks, and she looked more devastated than ever.

"You stole it," she said. "You really, truly stole it, didn't you?"

"I'm sorry, Marcy," he said again. "I was a dumb kid. But I mean, come on. Kids do dumb stuff all the time. And it's not like I stole the crown jewels. It's just a hair thing from the mall."

She expelled a single, incredulous chuckle. "A hair thing from the mall," she repeated. "Do you really think I'm going to believe that's what you thought?" She lifted the accessory between them. "These are diamonds, Max. Set in platinum. This comb was custom made for my great-grandmother, a gift from her husband on their anniversary. There's not another one like it in the world. It's worth *a fortune.*"

His stomach knotted at her assertion. Holy crow. He really had stolen the crown jewels. He'd had no idea he was grabbing something that valuable. How could he? The closest he'd ever been to fine jewelry was his mother's engagement ring—all one quarter carat of it. He wouldn't have known platinum from peanut butter when he was a kid. He wouldn't know it now. He started to apologize again, even more profusely than before, but she stopped him.

"When this went missing…" She shook her head. "When a lot of stuff went missing… When they told me you were the one who stole it all, I couldn't believe it." She looked at the jewelry nestled in her hand again. "But you did."

It took a minute for everything she'd said to sink in. Stole it *all*? he echoed to himself. He hadn't touched anything in that house besides that comb.

"What are you talking about?" he asked. "Stole all what? And just for the record," he added, "I didn't *steal* that comb. Not maliciously. I knew you were leaving Endicott soon, and I just wanted something to remember you by. It was on your dresser, so I just…took it. If I'd known what it really was, I never would have touched it."

"You stole it. You stole all of it."

There was that word again. "Stole *all* of what?" he demanded. Okay, maybe he had taken the comb without her permission—maybe he had stolen it, he made himself admit—but he hadn't realized he was taking anything of value. He'd just wanted a memento. That was it.

She expelled a soft, angry sound. "I can't believe you're denying it, when I'm standing here with the evidence in my hand."

"I'm not denying that," he told her, pointing to her hand. "I just admitted to it. But you seem to be accusing me of taking something else. And I didn't take anything else."

She was still looking at him as if he had committed the crime of the century. He simply did not understand why she was making such a big deal out of this after he'd explained himself. He could understand why she would still be angry with him. But she didn't even seem willing to consider the circumstances or his explanation. She'd already come to the conclusion that he was some kind of archvillain. When nothing could be further from the truth.

"Marcy, please," he said, more softly, less contentiously. "Just tell me what it is you think I did."

She expelled another one of those restless, bitter sighs, then dropped the hand holding the comb to her side. "I don't *think* you did anything. I *know* what you did. And my father went to prison because of it."

Whoa. Whoa, whoa, whoa. There was so much to unpack in that statement, Max didn't know where to begin.

"Your father is in prison?"

"He's out now. But he served five years of a seven year sentence for something he didn't do. Something he could have proven he didn't do if you hadn't stolen that safe from our house when we lived here."

"Safe?" he repeated, more confused now than ever. "What safe? I never stole a safe. I never even saw a safe."

"It was in my father's office. The one you went into that day."

"The one I walked maybe two feet into, just to look around," he said. "I was in a few other rooms that day, too, but I didn't take anything from any of them, either."

"Max, there's evidence. My parents had security cameras all over that house, and they have you on video inside, wandering around."

He shouldn't have been surprised that the Hanlons had security cameras, but he was. He supposed anyone with their kind of wealth would make sure their security was as tight as Fort Knox. Naturally, that wouldn't have occurred to him when he was a teenager, either.

Even so, he told her, "That's because I was inside, wandering around. We've already established that." Just where the hell was she going with this? Besides in circles? Because even if he was caught on video, there couldn't be any with him carrying around a safe he never even saw.

"The point is, they have you on video in the house," she repeated.

"Do they have me on video in the house carrying around the safe you're accusing me of taking?" he asked.

Her expression fell at that. "No. But you were there. And you just admitted to stealing this." Again with the hair comb.

"And I told you why. Because I was some love-sick kid who wanted to have something to remember the girl he liked by after she was gone. Why would I think it was worth a fortune if I'd seen you wearing it at school?"

Instead of accepting his explanation—again—she pulled herself up straight and glared at him. Almost as if she'd just reminded herself not to let him or his excuses sway her. "It had to be you," she said.

"My parents told me no one else was in the house at the time the safe went missing."

At the words *my parents told me*, things began to click into place for Max. He dropped his hands to his hips and only then recalled he was wearing nothing but a towel. He should have felt exposed and vulnerable. Instead, he just felt mad. Marcy noted the action, too, he saw, and her expression changed, growing a bit more moderate and a bit less certain. And maybe a little more... guilty? Good. She should feel guilty, being so sure of something so ridiculous after what the two of them had just shared. Hell, even if they hadn't just come together the way they had, she should know him better than that.

"Your parents told you that, huh?" he asked, a little more harshly than he intended. He couldn't help it. He couldn't understand how she could think the things about him that she was thinking. "And just exactly when did your parents tell you that?"

"My sophomore year in college," she said. "That's when they told all of us. Me, Remy, Percy and Mads."

"So...what? Four years after the fact? Why would they tell you that then?"

"It was right after my father was indicted," she said. "They had to tell us what was going on and why he didn't have the means to defend himself against charges of embezzling, fraud and extortion. The documents that would have cleared him were in that safe, along with my mother's most valuable jewelry." She held up the hair comb again. "Like this."

"That was on your dresser that day," Max reminded her. "And I already copped to that. I'm not going to cop to something I didn't do. And I didn't take a safe full of documents and jewelry."

For one brief, shining moment, she almost looked like she believed him. Then that moment shattered when she asked, "How were you able to afford to buy Mr. Bartok's business? How were you able to afford this place? How were your parents able to send your brothers and sisters to college on the wages of a teacher and a bowling-alley owner? All those things cost a lot of money. Just where did that money come from?"

Now Max was angry, too. He and his family might be working class, but that didn't mean they were ignorant. Or thieves. Or any of the other things she thought they were.

"Marcy, I know this is going to be an alien concept for someone like you, who's never worked a day in her life at any kind of *real* job—" Here, she grew even angrier, too. "—and who's never known what it's like to go without things," he continued before she could erupt. "But I've been working since I was fourteen years old. Sometimes two jobs at once. I saved every nickel I made so that I could start my own business someday and own my own home. My sister and brothers worked, too, as soon as they were old enough. And, hey, guess what? Even teachers and bowling-alley owners know how to plan for their and their kids' futures. Everything we have—everything *I* have—we've earned. I've earned. We didn't get it through the simple luck of birth the way you and your brothers did. And, hell, your parents, for that matter."

She looked like she wanted to blow up at him. But there was no way to defend herself from the truth. All she said was, quietly and evenly, "You did it."

"And how do you know it was me?" he asked again.

"I told you. My parents said—"

"No, how do *you* know, Marcy? Not your parents. Hell, they've always thought the worst of me. Of course, they'd accuse me of a crime before they'd even look at anyone else. How do *you* know I did it?"

She said nothing in response to his questions.

So Max continued, "*If* those things were actually stolen, it could have happened at any time. Before *or* after I was in your house. And what? Like

I'm the only person who was ever in your house? It couldn't have been any of the dozens of other people your family ever invited over? I was only in the place one time, since I was never allowed inside because your mom was worried that I—" Here, he made overly dramatic air quotes. "—might have mud on my shoes. Or maybe it was because your dad just didn't like having teenagers in the house. Even though Mr. Bartok, white Mr. Bartok," he made sure to clarify, "came and went as he pleased with his muddy shoes. And all four of you Hanlon kids had plenty of parties with your—" Again, he couldn't keep himself from pointing out the obvious, since Marcy seemed to be conveniently overlooking it. "—white teenage friends."

He stopped to give her a chance to interject any additional "evidence" she might have, or to defend her family. But she didn't say a word. She only continued to look at him with distress.

"So then maybe," Max continued, "your parents figured it must be me because of my long history of delinquent behavior. Except I don't have one. That would be your brothers, who were regular fixtures in the principal's office and the Endicott police station. Or hey, wait. I know. Maybe it's because I was the Black kid. Black kids are always stealing things. You don't even have to get them on video doing it to make those charges stick like glue."

Here, Marcy's expression changed drastically. Gone were the combativeness and coldness. In their place was…something else. Something Max couldn't quite read.

Not until she said, "You're not Black. Your father is white."

Of all the hurtful things she'd said tonight—and she'd said a lot of hurtful things—that one was the worst. Because it completely erased half of his heritage. And that erased him. She didn't even see him for who he really was. She probably never had. And that, more than anything else, assured him that anything he thought they'd had was a complete sham. How could she ever really care for him when she didn't even see him for who he was?

"You know what my real name is?" he asked her.

She looked confused but said nothing.

So he continued, "Max is my nickname. My full first name is Makisenyo. It's Amharic for Tuesday, which is what day I was born on. My brother Gabe has an Ethiopian name, too. Gebre, also Amharic. Amharic is my mother's native language. It's what she and her family speak in her country. Which, in case I didn't mention it, is Ethiopia.

"So I'm Black, Marcy," he assured her. "Ask

anybody. Ask your folks. See what they say. And while you're at it, ask them what *really* happened to that safe that went missing. I think you should go," he concluded before she could say anything else.

Not that she looked like she had any idea what else to say. Mostly, she looked like she wanted to cry. Max didn't blame her. He felt like crying, too.

"I'll call you a ride," he said. "But then you and I are done."

He'd figured she would be glad to hear it, since she obviously thought him capable of thievery and lying. Instead, her eyes filled with tears again. Max clenched his jaw tight and went to his living room to retrieve his phone. If she wanted to cry, it wasn't because of anything he'd done. It was because she'd assumed things about him that weren't true, even though she should have known better.

She'd clearly never known him at all. Worse than that, he'd never known her at all, either. He'd thought she was perfect. All these years, she had been the ideal of…of everything. But now he knew better. Marcy Hanlon was nothing but a common fraud.

It was all Marcy could do to make it back to the hotel before she fell apart. The moment the door to her room was shut behind her, though, she did exactly that. For a long time, she only lay curled in a ball on her bed and cried. She didn't think about anything that had happened or been said that night. She only let herself feel the repercussions from it all. And, boy, were there repercussions. Her whole body shook with uncontrollable sobs, until her head was pounding and her face felt numb. The sun was rising outside before she finally ran out of tears. Only then did she let herself replay any of the night before in her head.

What had she done? Oh, god. *What had she done?*

Everything felt wrong this morning. Everything. The sun streaming through the window was hard and glaring. The breeze was dry and harsh. Instead of the fragrance of the garden flowers, all she could smell was the acrid aroma of a truck idling outside. Even the birds seemed to mock her with tweets of *twit twit twit* and *ninny ninny ninny*.

What had happened last night?

It had all started off so well. When she'd come down the stairs to find Max waiting for her, she'd thought about how that was what it would have been like if she'd stayed in Endicott and gone to the prom with him. His dilapidated truck had only firmed the image better. They'd actually passed their old high school on the way to Max's place, and she'd almost been surprised when they didn't pull into the lot for the dance. Then picking apples and sharing dinner with him... The way he fed her with such gentleness and sweetness... And then, later, when they'd come together with such passion and such joy, when he'd murmured that he loved her, and she'd almost thought she loved him, too.

How could she have said the things she said to him last night? How could she have felt the things she felt?

But he'd had her great-grandmother's comb, she reminded herself. What else was she supposed to have thought and said?

And he'd explained how and why he came into its possession, she reminded herself further. Because he knew she would be leaving Endicott soon and wanted something to remember her—

Something in Marcy's belly clenched tight as a sudden realization and a forgotten memory tried to wedge themselves into her brain. She jackknifed up from the bed to sit on its edge. Then she closed her eyes and made herself concentrate. Hard.

If Max had taken the comb as a memento shortly before her departure from Endicott because he knew she'd be leaving soon, that meant he took it *after* the time her father claimed the safe was stolen. She couldn't remember if there had been a time stamp on the video her father played for them during that phone call, but those things could be altered or deleted, couldn't they? And if Max had taken the comb from the jewelry box on her dresser, then that meant…

Oh, god. Oh, no. Oh…fuh…uh…dge.

Marcy made herself remember something she truly hadn't thought about since leaving Endicott when she was a teenager. Like so many other things she had made herself forget—because they had just been too painful to recall after the family's move—she had forgotten until now how her great-grandmother's comb couldn't have been in the safe when it was stolen after the first of the year, when her father had told them all it was taken. That was because the comb hadn't been in the safe since before Christmas. She'd been so overcome last night by the pain of what she'd been certain was Max's betrayal that it was only now registering in her brain how he'd told her he took the comb from her jewelry box. In the heat of the moment, she'd thought he was just trying to cover his crime. But now…

Now she remembered something she really should have recalled before now.

She'd been enchanted by her great-grandmother's comb since she was a very little girl, the first time her mother showed it to her. Once she knew the combination to the safe—the one Remy revealed to all of the siblings after he saw their father open it once—she'd "borrowed" the comb from time to time. Just to wear it in her bedroom, because it had made her feel like a princess. But she'd always returned it before her parents knew it was missing.

Except for once. The night of the holiday concert.

She'd realized she was still wearing it when she entered the house after Amanda's parents dropped her off afterward, and her mother had nearly caught her wearing it. She'd stuffed it into her pocket just in time, then into her jewelry box once she got to her room. She'd had every intention of returning it to the safe as soon as she could. But she'd never had a chance. First had come the holiday season, with all its bustle and extra people around, then had come the new school term and all its ensuing excitement and chaos, then a million other things that replaced the memory of the comb in her jewelry box. She'd been a typical teenager with a capricious attention span. She'd just…forgotten…to put the comb back where it belonged.

It hadn't been in the safe when the safe was stolen, Marcy realized now. Not if, as her father claimed, the safe had been stolen after the first of the year. It had been in her jewelry box. Exactly where Max said he found it.

Nausea rolled through her belly again when she recalled all the things she'd said to him the night before. Not just about the theft, but about…about everything else, too. Her words—and a whole lot more—were unforgiveable. But if there was even the tiniest chance that Max could see past her horribleness to at least allow her to apologize and make an effort to explain, she had to try.

Before doing that, though, she needed to find out the truth about what really happened to the safe and why her parents had been so certain Max was the thief. Not that she didn't already have some clue about that, but she needed and deserved to know the facts. And so did Max.

As she rose from bed and went to the bathroom to wash her face, their final exchange came back to haunt her. When she'd told him he wasn't Black, she hadn't meant it the way he thought she had. She hadn't intended to deny any part of him. He wouldn't be Max without *all* of his heritage. She'd just been trying to…what? Defend him, in spite of their dispute at the time? But defend him from what, exactly? And what kind of defense had she been offering him, anyway? That by somehow reassuring him that, hey, since he had some whiteness in him, he couldn't be as bad as her father thought he was? Had she actually told him that? That made her just as bad as her father was. Maybe worse. At least her father didn't make any secret about his own bias.

But she wasn't biased. Was she?

There was a part of her that honestly wasn't sure how to answer that question. And that, more than anything else she'd had to think about this morning, might just be the toughest thing of all for her to consider.

She looked at the phone sitting on the bed beside her. Gingerly, she grasped it and fed in the code to unlock it. And then, even more gingerly, she scrolled to her mother's phone number and hit Call.

Chapter Nine

Thursday morning, Max awoke to the scent of Marcy on the pillow beside him, a fragrance redolent of roses and peonies and peaches. For long moments, he only lay there with his eyes closed, replaying every second of the night before and wishing it had ended differently. Like, maybe waking this morning to find her still in bed beside him. He could go in late to work and make an Ethiopian breakfast for her. Maybe some *fit-fit* with the leftover injera from last night and a little yogurt and peppers on the side. Then, what the hell, he could blow off work entirely and the two of them could spend the whole day together. Today was Thursday, the biggest day of the Welcome Back, Bob Comet Festival, because tonight, the comet would be making its closest pass to the planet. There would be tons of stuff to do, all over town. He couldn't remember the last time he'd taken an entire day off from work, and to spend it doing nothing but enjoy it with someone he lo— With someone he cared about, would have been the best gift in the world.

Instead, when he opened his eyes, the bed beside him was empty, save for a single strand of auburn hair clinging to the sheet. All he had left of Marcy. He opened his palm over the curl and inhaled the lingering fragrance of her. Had it not been for those two things, he might have been able to convince himself that last night—all of it—was a dream. The first part pretty much had been. He couldn't have orchestrated anything more perfect than their dinner and the way they'd come together afterward. What happened after that, though, was a nightmare. One he wasn't likely to wake up from anytime soon.

He pushed himself onto his elbows, looked out the window and realized he was, in fact, late to work, because sunlight was slanting in. He didn't care. He felt like crap. But if feeling like crap was an excuse to skip work, then he might as well forget about going in for a long time.

He kicked off the covers and pulled on his clothes,

then went to the kitchen to make coffee. Thankfully, he didn't have to go to Hanlon House for anything today. And even if he did, he would have sent someone else to do it. He wasn't sure he would be able to go back over there for the foreseeable future. The garden he'd always loved was just going to be a reminder of how badly things had turned out with him and the one woman he'd been so sure was perfect for him. Who he'd been so sure was just plain perfect period. Hah. What an idiot he'd been. The whole Hanlon family tree was just blighted. He didn't know why he didn't realize that a long time ago.

He spent the rest of the day on autopilot, working in the office instead of out in the field, because he was just too exhausted for physical labor. He'd put off enough paperwork to keep him busy for the bulk of the day, and he locked the place up tight once everyone else had gone home. Then he picked up his phone to text everyone he knew, to see if they were busy or if they wanted to go grab a beer or something. Even though, with tonight being prime time for Bob, everyone would be busy. It was the night every kid in town who'd been born during the year of the comet's last visit would be making wishes for next time, the night everyone who'd made wishes fifteen years ago would be looking for them to come true, if they hadn't come true already. Lucky them.

Max winced when he realized that, like his two best friends, his wish had come true this year, too. Marcy Hanlon did indeed see him as someone other than the kid who took care of her parents' yard fifteen years ago. She saw him as a thief. And as a liar. And as someone who was beneath her. Lucky him, too. He just hadn't considered the possibility, fifteen years ago, that his luck this year would be bad.

Sure enough, everyone he knew did have plans. Chance was spending the evening with his new family—he'd promised his niece and nephew they could stay up late and make wishes, too, even though they weren't comet kids, since maybe Bob would be in a generous mood and grant their wishes, anyway. But, hey, Max was welcome to join them. Felix, he had been surprised to learn, had plans with his neighbor, Rory, with whom things seemed to be going a lot better than they had a few days ago, but, fine, if Max wanted to be a fifth wheel—hint, hint—he could hang with them. Everyone in Max's family was together grilling at Zach's house, and hey, why didn't he come over, too? But Max wasn't really up for a crowd—even a crowd of three or four—so he'd told his friends and family he'd just catch them next time.

After that, he thought maybe he would just go somewhere by himself where he could shake an angry fist at the night sky and demand an explanation from Bob about why everyone else's wishes were making them so happy while his had gone so badly awry. What had he done to make the comet so mad? He was a good guy. He worked hard and paid his taxes. He lived and let live. He was kind to animals and children. Just what had he done that had soured the universe to the point where it didn't think he deserved happiness?

Then he decided he was being maudlin and ridiculous and needed to take himself home. Home to the house where he'd be assailed by reminders of the night before the minute he walked through the front door. Where there would be something of Marcy in almost every corner. Hell, every time he drove up the drive and saw the apple orchard, he'd think of her. Every time he made something for dinner in his kitchen or even ate Ethiopian food, he'd remember her. Every time he lay down in bed at night, he'd be reminded of—

Ah, hell. At this rate, he wouldn't ever be able to spend time in his house again. Marcy would be everywhere.

Including his front porch, he saw, when he pulled to a stop in front of his house that evening. She was sitting on the wicker swing at the far end, her dress a splash of pink and pale yellow against the slashes of orange and lavender in the sunset behind her. And Sodo—that traitor—was sitting in the swing beside her, loving the way she was stroking her. He couldn't help remembering how he'd asked Marcy last night if she wanted to sit outside like this, before they— After dinner, he quickly corrected himself. But they never made it outside because instead they—

He threw the truck into Park and climbed out, then slammed the door with a little more force than was necessary. "What are you doing here?" he asked by way of a greeting.

He couldn't help himself. He was still mad about a lot of the things she'd said the night before. He still couldn't believe she would consider him a villain. He still couldn't believe she'd tried to white-wash who he was.

He still couldn't believe she wasn't perfect.

She eased herself off the swing, much to Sodo's disappointment, and covered the distance between it and the porch stairs. But she didn't come down to join him. The fact that she kept herself above him like that only reminded him of the way she'd put herself above him last night, too, something that brought his anger to a simmer.

"I owe you an apology," she told him point-blank,

surprising him. Before he could say more, she added, "I'm sorry, Max. I never should have said the things I said last night."

He took a few slow steps forward, stopping at the foot of the stairs. She still didn't come down to meet him. Not even halfway. He noticed, too, that she'd told him she shouldn't have said what she said last night. She wasn't apologizing for feeling the way she felt and believing the way she believed.

"No, you shouldn't have," he replied. "But it's not what you said that did the most damage, Marcy. It's that you believed every word that came out of your mouth. You really thought I could be a thief. Even after all the time we spent together this week. Even after we—"

He halted himself before finishing that sentence, but not, he could tell by her expression, before she knew exactly what he was going to say.

"And as if that wasn't enough," he hurried on, "you tried to erase half of who I am to make yourself feel better about being with me."

She said nothing to defend herself from his charges. Which could only mean he was right. He ought to feel smug about that. Instead, he felt sick.

"Can we talk?" she asked softly. "Please?"

"We don't have anything to talk about."

She grew more distressed at his reply. "You're wrong, Max. Okay, maybe you don't have to talk about anything," she quickly amended. "But I do."

"I don't want to do this, Marcy," he said flatly. "It's been a hell of a day, after a hell of a night, and I'm exhausted. You said what you said, you thought what you thought, you felt what you felt, and I don't think there's anything you can say or do now that will make any of that go away. You should just go back to your—"

"I was wrong," she interjected. "Horribly, horribly wrong. About everything."

He stopped talking at her admission. But he didn't stop being mad. Yeah, she had been wrong. But that didn't change the fact that she had thought the worst of him for no good reason. That she had tried to reconstruct him into something he wasn't. That she had turned out to be someone so…imperfect.

When he said nothing in response to her statement, she sighed heavily, then continued, "I called my mother last night. I asked her to go somewhere that my father wasn't and call me back. It took some convincing, but she finally did. Then I asked her what really happened to the safe fifteen years ago."

Max said nothing. But instead of relaxing at her admission, the resentment inside him only compounded.

"That took even more convincing," Marcy continued. "At first, she insisted that everything my father told me and my brothers about you was true. She reminded me of the video and how no one had been in the house besides you at the time. I told her she was lying, that I'd been back in Endicott for almost a week and had been spending time with you, and I knew you weren't the kind of person, then or now, who could do what she and my father accused you of." She hesitated, as if she was weighing whether or not she should say something else. But all she did was stammer. "Then she… She…"

She paused, then wound her fingers together tight. Her gaze ricocheted off his and landed on something in the night sky above him. Finally, she spoke again. "Then she started to cry. She said my father would be furious with her if she told me what really happened, and then she made me promise to never say anything to him about our conversation before she would tell me what really happened."

Max remembered how timid Mrs. Hanlon had always seemed to him, regardless of where she was or who she was with. But whenever he saw her with her husband, she seemed especially cowed. He honestly couldn't remember her ever even speaking when Marcy's father was present.

"And did your mother tell you what really happened?"

At this, Marcy's gaze connected with his again. But only for a couple of seconds. Then she dropped it to the ground and nodded. "Yes. She did."

"Did she tell you it was the thieving Black kid?"

This time, when Marcy's gaze connected with Max's, it held firm. Something fierce and bitter gleamed in her eyes. "No. She told me it was my brother Remy."

Of all the people she could have named, and in spite of his general disdain for the Hanlons, it never would have occurred to Max that one of her brothers would be the culprit.

"What?" he said, his disbelief overtaking anything else that might have come to mind.

"It was Remy," she said again, her voice a little softer now.

She finally made her way down the steps to where he was, though she halted when there was still a good bit of space between them. Even so, she was close enough now that he could see smudges of color beneath her eyes that told him she hadn't slept any better than he had last night, and that she'd been crying. A lot.

"Can we please talk?" she asked again.

Max would be lying if he said he didn't want to

hear the rest of this story. So he nodded silently. But instead of sweeping a hand toward the swing she'd just left, where they would have been infinitely more comfortable, he strode past her to take a seat on the bottom step, as far away from her as he could. He didn't want to be comfortable. And he didn't want her to be comfortable, either. Whatever she had to tell him was bound to make things worse before making them better. Hell, the way he felt right now, it sounded like whatever she was going to say would only make things worse between them, period. She hesitated only a moment before sweeping her dress under her and sitting on the opposite side of the same step, as far away from Max as she could be, too.

"Remy got into some trouble his first year at Penn," she began. "Drinking, drugs, gambling, you name it. I knew nothing about it," she clarified. "As far as I knew, he was excelling the same way he did all through high school. But something happened once he got away from home…"

Here, she inhaled a deep breath and looked at the sky again. "No, I know exactly what happened to him. It happened to me, too. When you grow up in a household that was as authoritarian as ours was, where you're never given any freedom and watched like a hawk, and where there are no healthy examples of how to cope, you get into trouble the minute you're out of that environment."

Like partying to excess, Max thought, the way Marcy had. Like dating people who weren't good for you. Like marrying a guy who's no better at being a husband to you than your father was at being a husband to your mother. He tried to be sympathetic. He couldn't imagine what it must have been like for her to have parents like the ones she had. Especially when she'd been living in such a grand, glorious home and had seemingly lacked for nothing. The Hanlons had been pillars of the community. They'd set a standard in town that a lot of others had tried to emulate. In a lot of towns-folks' eyes, they had been an ideal to look up to. If they'd all realized just how cold and controlling the family dynamics had actually been, they prob-ably would have been pretty surprised.

Max might have come from a working-class household that struggled to make ends meet some-times, but it had been filled with love and trust and respect. His parents had never made him or any of his siblings feel stifled or disrespected. On the contrary, they'd always been made to feel that they could do or be whatever they wanted, and they'd been given the freedom to explore and grow and thrive. Even though he'd seen for himself what kind of man Lionel Remington Hanlon IV was, it had never occurred to him, at fifteen, what kind of damage that could do to a family that had to live with his dictatorial ways every single day of their life.

"By the time Remy was a junior at Penn," Marcy continued, "which would have been the year you and I were sophomores at Endicott High, he was in so deep to so many people and owed so much money and so many favors, there was no way he could dig himself out. He'd been working over the summers at my father's investment company since he was sixteen, and he was smart enough to learn how to cook the books. He'd been embezzling money to pay off his debts for years—I think, maybe, even before he started college—but he didn't stop doing the things that got him into trouble in the first place, so it just became this vicious cycle."

"So he stole the family safe with the jewelry, too," Max mused.

Marcy nodded.

"What happened to it?" he asked.

"It's gone," she said flatly. "It's been gone for fifteen years. There's pretty much no chance it will ever be recovered now." She attempted a smile, but it didn't quite materialize. "Except for the comb," she added. "Ironically, I still have my great-grand-mother's comb, thanks to—"

"Thanks to my stealing it," he said harshly.

Her back bowed, and she suddenly looked exhausted. Quietly, she said, "Had you let me finish, I was going to say 'thanks to *my* stealing it.'"

Now Max was the one to sit up straighter. "What are you talking about?"

She leaned back against the porch banister. "My mother wouldn't let me wear the comb to the holiday concert because she said it was too valuable and I might lose it. The only reason I was able to wear it that night was because I took it from the safe myself without her knowing. Long story short, I put it in my jewelry box and forgot all about it and didn't get a chance to put it back before you…picked it up," she said, making a clear effort to avoid any reference to theft. "I had truly forgotten about that until you mentioned finding it in my jewelry box. At the time you said it last night, I thought you were lying about that, too. It wasn't until I got back to the hotel that I remembered what I did. It wasn't you who took it—not the first time, anyway—it was me. Yet another apology I owe you."

Well, thanks for that measly bone, Marcy Hanlon.

"So let me get this straight," he said. "You accused me of stealing something you yourself had already stolen?"

"I didn't steal it," she said.

"You just said you stole it."

"You know what I meant. I didn't steal it—I borrowed it. But, yes. I did it without permission, and it was lousy of me to accuse you of doing something I did myself. When I accused you last night, I thought you'd stolen a lot more than the comb."

"Don't remind me," he said bitterly.

She uttered a soft, strangled sound at his remark. Even more softly this time, she told him, "I know the things I said last night are unforgiveable." Her eyes filled with tears as she spoke. "I can't believe I said what I did. I can't believe I was the person I was last night at all. I don't blame you for hating me. I hate myself."

Instead of feeling vindicated by her words, all Max wanted to do was tell her he didn't hate her. Because he didn't. Which kind of surprised him, but there it was all the same. Before he could respond at all, she continued.

"So I don't expect you to forgive me, and I don't expect you to ever want to see me again after tonight. But I hope you'll at least let me finish explaining and do my best to apologize to you."

"Fine," he said wearily. "Say what you need to say."

Then she could go, and maybe—maybe—someday he could forget this whole sorry chapter of his life.

"When Remy took the safe," she told him, "he didn't even care about the documents that were in there and ended up trashing them. They were records my father always made sure to keep at home because they documented everything he ever did for his clients. Those records would have countered what Remy did with the records at the office, and they would have eventually pointed a finger at Remy, too. But Remy didn't even know that. He stole the whole safe to make it look like someone else just grabbed it and ran off with it."

Here, her gaze met Max's again. "I'm pretty sure he assumed everyone would blame you. You or Mr. Bartok or Mrs. Mazzoni. But mostly you."

He repeated what he said the night before. "Because I was the Black kid."

She closed her eyes. And she nodded. "Yeah. Because you were the Black kid. To my family, you were an easy target."

"To a lot of people, I would've been an easy target," he said. "I still am. There. Fixed that for you."

She opened her eyes again. "I am sorry, Max.

What's worse is that my parents suspected all along that Remy was the one who took it. They knew he was in trouble and figured he'd taken it to fence the jewelry. But they couldn't have anyone knowing what their son had done, so they didn't report the theft to the police. Even though the jewelry was worth a fortune, it was still a smaller price to pay than having the family name and reputation dragged through the mud. My father didn't know yet about Remy's embezzling. So he didn't worry that much about the documents inside. His primary concern—his only concern—was saving face. So even when he was accused of the embezzlement, even after Remy admitted what he had done, my father didn't turn in his son. Remy still had his whole life ahead of him. My father was nearing retirement. He knew he'd go off to some cushy white-collar facility for a few years, then he and my mom could drop off the grid, and that would be the end of it."

"So, what? Remy just gets off scot-free for everything he did?" Max asked.

She nodded. "Pretty much, yeah. Unless you want to count him having to live with the knowledge of his deeds for the rest of his life."

"Like he's going to be bothered by any of that."

"No, probably not," she agreed. "But for what

it's worth, my folks hired a watchdog for him after they discovered what he'd done, a big, burly guy named Buzz who never let him out of his sight and made sure he attended all his various anonymous groups and got clean and stayed out of trouble. And from all reports, he has stayed clean and out of trouble ever since then."

"And now he's a fine, upstanding investment broker in Rhode Island who spends the weekends racing yachts with his son. Who says crime doesn't pay?"

She pulled her knees up in front of her and wrapped her arms around her legs. It was a position Max could only liken to defensiveness. "My family—all of us—have been awful to you, Max. I'm sorry. And I have no idea what to say or do to make amends for that. But I wish you would let me try."

It wasn't up to Marcy to make amends for her family, Max knew. Frankly, he didn't give a damn about her family. He didn't give a damn about her, either, he told himself. She'd still been quick to assume the worst of him. She'd still tried to turn him into something he wasn't. She'd still disappointed him in so many ways by not being the person he thought she was.

"Don't bother," he told her. "It's not important."

"It's important to me."

"Right. Sure it is," he said flippantly.

She looked genuinely confused by his reaction. "I don't understand why you're being like this. I'm trying to do what's right. I'm trying to extend some kind of olive branch that will make things okay between us."

"Marcy, I can safely say things between us will never be okay."

Now she looked devastated. "Max, you're not even giving me a chance. That's not fair."

He stood. He wasn't about to debate fairness with her. Instead, he told her, "Okay, you've given me the scoop and apologized. Thanks. Now if you'll excuse me, I need to make myself some dinner and get to bed. Early day tomorrow and all that."

She stood, too, looking at him incredulously. "That's really it?" she asked. "You're really not even going to try to work this out?"

"What's there to work out?" he asked. "Your brother is a thief and a liar. Your parents and other brothers are liars. You believed all of them over me, even after you had to realize they were far more likely to not be telling the truth than I was." He climbed the steps, turning at the top to look down on her this time. "You're not the perfect human being I always thought you were, Marcy. End of story."

She started to laugh, albeit a bit humorlessly,

at that last comment, then must have realized he was serious. "Wait, what?" she asked. "You actually thought I was perfect?"

"Yeah, I actually thought you were perfect," he told her. "You were always perfect. Back when we were kids, you were perfect. When we were teenagers, you were perfect. You were supposed to still be perfect now. But you're not. And I'm just not sure how to deal with that."

As he spoke, her mouth gradually opened in what he could only interpret as disbelief. "Perfect?" she echoed again. "My god, why would you even think that about me?"

Now Max was the incredulous one. How could she even ask that? "Because everything about you was always perfect," he said. "The way you looked, the way you acted, the way you treated me. You were always the epitome of excellence when we were kids. You were the ideal human being, the exemplar of what every person should strive to be. You were the one girl on the planet—the one woman on the planet—who was…perfect."

As he spoke, he knew he sounded like an idiot. No, he sounded like a fifteen-year-old kid who was so besotted that he didn't even know how to express himself properly. He didn't care. He wanted Marcy to know just how deeply she'd disappointed him.

How deeply she'd hurt him. And, honestly, once the words were out of his mouth, he was glad he'd said them and put them out in the world. Finally.

She shook her head slowly. "Max, I'm not perfect. I was never perfect. I'm as far from perfect as a human being can be. I've made so many mistakes, done so many things I wish I could undo. For you to think I'm perfect, that I should even strive to be perfect... That's so unfair."

"What's unfair about it?"

"No one is perfect," she said.

"You were, once," he told her.

"And that's the thing you find most unforgivable," she said. As a statement, not a question. "That I'm not perfect."

Max said nothing.

"And that's why you won't even try to work this out. Because I'm not the ideal you always thought I was. That you always wanted me to be. That *you* always made me to be in your head."

Still, Max remained silent.

"You're a bigot, too," she told him.

He expelled a single, humorless chuckle. "No, I'm not."

"Yeah, you are. You expect me to be something I'm not and have never been for the simple reason that it suits your worldview and makes you feel better about yourself. You've had this obstinate, irrational opinion of me for years, even though you've seen plenty of proof to the contrary, and now you're upset that I'm not the thing you insist I should be, something I never was in the first place."

"Marcy, that makes no sense."

"Oh, it makes total sense." She shook her head again. "Clearly, I'm not the only one who's been wrong in my thinking about someone. I'm just the only one who admitted it and apologized for it and tried to make amends."

She waited for him to respond. But Max really had no idea what to say. He wasn't a bigot. Was he?

Now she nodded, her expression resolute. "Well, okay, then. I guess you're right. You and I have nothing to talk about. Not anymore."

She descended from the bottom step to the ground and began to walk away, without saying another word. She didn't even look at him. He had no idea where she was going. There wasn't another vehicle in sight, so she'd obviously gotten a ride here. His driveway to the highway was nearly a half-mile long and wasn't lit at all. Not that there had been a vehicle out there, either.

"Where are you going?" he called after her.

But she remained silent. As she'd just told him, they had nothing to talk about. Instead, she took her phone out of her pocket and tapped the screen to bring it to life. He saw its hazy glow in her hand as she made her way into the growing darkness. She was obviously ordering a ride, presumably to meet her at the end of his long, long drive. He told himself to let her go, that she was perfectly safe. But even feeling the way he did about her, he couldn't quite let himself.

"Marcy, wait," he called after her. "At least let your ride come to the house. You don't have to walk down to the highway."

But she never looked back and just kept walking. Muttering a ripe oath under his breath, Max followed her on foot, keeping his distance, all the way down the drive until he saw her stop at the road. Not five minutes later, a car bearing rideshare logos stopped for her. She climbed into the back seat, and the car took off. A moment later, it passed again in the other direction, having made a U-turn somewhere to head back into town. Marcy must have told him not to pull into Max's driveway to do it. She really didn't want to have anything to do with him anymore.

But that was good, right? he told himself as he turned and made his way back toward the house. There obviously wasn't any future for them. There never had been. She'd been wrong about him, and he'd been wrong about her. End of story.

And yet... And yet...

Those two words were still pounding in his head when he climbed the stairs to his front porch. And yet it didn't feel quite like the end of their story.

As Sodo leaped down from the swing to join him, Max turned and looked up at the sky, finding Bob immediately. The comet had granted his wish, he knew. And yet...

And yet.

Chapter Ten

"Why, if it isn't little Marcy Hanlon, as I live and breathe."

Marcy looked up from her breakfast in the Hanlon House dining room on Friday morning to see Mrs. Pendleton Barclay, Endicott's society grand dame, smiling down at her. Okay, well, not so much smiling down, since Mrs. Barclay probably didn't even top five feet these days, but she was smiling. She was a study in pastels, from her yellow top and green sweater to her blue cat-eye glasses and pink hair. Marcy smiled back at the vision. Everyone in town had a soft spot for Mrs. Barclay, even the ones who'd been absent for years, like her.

"Hi, Mrs. Barclay, how are you?" Marcy replied.

"I'm fine, dear. Just surprised we haven't run into each other before now. I was hoping to get to speak to you."

"Well, this is a busy time for Endicott, after all," Marcy replied. "And for you, too, I imagine, what with the Galaxy Ball tonight."

The ball tonight, she echoed to herself. The one she and Max were supposed to have attended together. Not that that was going to happen now. Not that anything more between them was going to happen now. Or ever.

The older woman glanced meaningfully at the empty chair to Marcy's right, then back at Marcy again, silently angling for an invitation to join her. The last thing Marcy wanted at the moment was to have to feign cheerfulness when her life was going down in flames around her...again. She still hadn't quite processed everything that had happened between her and Max this week, still hadn't been able to figure out how everything had gone so terribly wrong. And she still didn't know what to do about any of it.

Even so, she swept her hand to the right and said, "Do you have a few minutes to join me?"

Mrs. Barclay's smile was dazzling. "I'd love to. Thank you."

Marcy still remembered the big bash Mrs. Barclay threw at the last Welcome Back, Bob Comet Festival fifteen years ago, and how much fun it had been for the youngest generation of comet kids to be invited to such a swanky event. Although Marcy's family might have been the wealthiest in town, her parents hadn't entertained very often, and when they did, they never included the Hanlon offspring. Maybe Mrs. Barclay's house hadn't been as large or as old or as stately as the Hanlons', but it had been every bit as luxurious. And it had been far more welcoming, with personal touches everywhere, and a whole aura of warm invitation the Hanlons' house had lacked. She remembered the big ballroom, its ceiling painted with a mural of the cosmos, Comet Bob front and center, and how she and her friends Amanda and Claire had sat at a table on one side, taking it all in.

Mostly, though, Marcy recalled looking at Max, who'd been sitting with Felix and Chance and Chance's older brother, Logan. She'd never seen any of them in suits before, and Max's had clearly been a hand-me-down from a cousin or friend, because it hadn't fitted him at all. Not just in size, but in mien, either. As handsome as she'd thought him in it, ill-fitting or no, Max just wasn't the suit-wearing type. Not then, not now. It had somehow seemed wrong back then, seeing him in something that just wasn't...him.

She remembered again how he told her he always thought she was perfect. Something that wasn't her, either. They'd both made mistakes about each other—in the past and now. But where she was at least willing to try to do whatever it took to move forward—because she very much would have liked to move forward with Max—he couldn't get past the fact that she wasn't the perfect paragon of his dreams. And perfect was something Marcy would never be, even if she wanted to try.

He'd told her he loved her Wednesday night. She knew she had heard that correctly. But now she realized it wasn't her that he loved. He loved the idea of her that he'd created and nurtured in his head since they were kids.

Mrs. Barclay scooted forward in her chair just as a passing busboy approached, and she called him over by name and asked if he wouldn't mind very much bringing her another cup of tea, please. He nodded with a smile and told her he'd be right back, then went off to fetch one. The boy looked to be about fifteen. Marcy wondered if he was a comet kid who would be attending the ball tonight.

Mrs. Barclay smiled at Marcy and, as if reading her mind, she said, "That's Dante. He was born the last time Bob came around. He'll be at the party tonight."

"Mrs. Barclay, I think you must keep track of every kid in town who's born in a comet year," Marcy said. "I remember when I came to your party last time, you knew every single one of us by name."

"Well, I've been here for seven of Bob's visits," she said. "You might say I'm his official registrar at this point."

Marcy remembered Max telling her the town had celebrated Mrs. Barclay's ninetieth birthday in June. Ninety was divisible by fifteen. That meant Mrs. Barclay—

"Yes, I'm a comet kid, too, dear," she said, reading her mind again. "Except in my day, we called ourselves 'children of the comet.' I guess that got too old-fashioned-sounding, though. Who knows? In another ninety years, comet kids will be calling themselves something else more suited to the times."

Marcy was smiling now, too. "It never occurred to me that you might have been born in a year of the comet. I don't know why. It makes perfect sense, though, why you've always thrown the party and had us all over. It's nice of you."

She waved a hand airily. "It's nice of all you young people to humor me."

Dante returned with her tea, told Mrs. Barclay he was looking forward to tonight, then returned to his duties. As she unwrapped her tea bag to dunk it in the water, she eyed Marcy pointedly.

"You're coming tonight, too, yes?" she asked.

Marcy had scrapped her plans to attend the gala last night, the minute she'd seen the way Max was looking at her after she called him a bigot. Which maybe had been a little too harsh on her part, but she hadn't been able to help it. He was a bigot of sorts, turning his back on her because she strayed from his expectations and preconceptions of her and wasn't—gasp—perfect. Maybe he was right that she hadn't seen him as honestly as she should have. But she realized that now, and she was working on fixing it. But he hadn't seen her as honestly as he should have, either. And he wouldn't even admit it or try to work on fixing his views. So, no. There was no reason for Marcy to go to the party tonight. The last thing she wanted was to see everyone excited about the wishes they'd just made or the ones they'd made last time and how they'd come true. Marcy's wish wasn't coming true. There was no way it would now, with things being the way they were between her and Max. Bob had let her down in a big way. There was nothing for her to be celebrating tonight.

"I haven't decided yet," she said, dodging the question, for now.

But Mrs. Barclay would clearly have none of it. "What? Why not? You have to come. All the comet kids *and* children of the comet will be there. Some have come from literally the other side of the world to be here."

Bucky Klopnik, Marcy concluded. She'd heard earlier this week that her former classmate was calling Australia home these days.

"I know, but—"

"No *buts*," Mrs. Barclay said decisively. "You're coming."

In spite of all the ickiness that had been coiling inside her for two days, Marcy smiled. "Yes, ma'am," she replied. But she still wasn't sure what she would do.

"Now then," Mrs. Barclay said, "tell me how your family is doing. I haven't heard a word about your mother or father for years. Or your brothers. None of us has. It's like they've fallen off the face of the earth."

Which was exactly how they all wanted to keep it, Marcy thought. She quickly gave Mrs. Barclay the highlights—the ones that *didn't* include her father's indictment, conviction and prison time, and focused instead on her parents' retirement in

Panama—and told her where her three brothers had landed and what they were doing.

"And how about you, dear?" Mrs. Barclay asked. "When is your next book coming out?"

It was a question that had come up every time she'd seen an old acquaintance in passing this week, but Marcy still had no idea how to answer it. There was a part of her that had hoped by coming home to her roots for the festival and reliving what had been one of the few highlights of her youth, she might be inspired in some way, and that ideas and words would just come flowing into her brain. There must be as many stories in the community right now as there were people, and she'd been vaguely optimistic that at least a few of them might find their way into her brain for her to write about. But her idea well had been drier this week than it had been in her entire life. She was beginning to think she just didn't have any stories left to tell.

"I'm kind of on hiatus," she told Mrs. Barclay evasively.

Mrs. Barclay seemed way more interested in that statement than she should have been. "Really? I was always under the impression that people who wrote books did so because they couldn't *not* write books. As if it were an obsession of sorts."

"It was, in the beginning," Marcy admitted. "But everyone needs a little break from their livelihood sometimes. I'll get back to it."

Eventually, she added to herself. Probably. At some point. Whenever her damn muse felt like coming back from wherever the hell it was muses went when they wanted to torture their creators. The little jerks.

"Well, I hope you come back to writing soon. I've very much enjoyed your books." She arrowed her silver eyebrows down a bit. "Although I thought the last two could have used a little…polishing."

And *poof* went Marcy's delusion that maybe her readers had been able to see past the lack of Marcella Robillard in the stories and still enjoy the books.

"They were still good," Mrs. Barclay quickly reassured her when she must have detected Marcy's disappointment. "Just not quite…you."

Not quite you. It was a phrase that had been tumbling through Marcy's head a lot this week. Probably because it was so meaningless. She didn't even know what was supposed to be her. Who was she? Marcy Hanlon, Midwestern teenager? Marcella Hanlon, urban party girl? Marcella Robillard, continental novelist and viscountess? Marcy Hanlon Robillard, washed-up everything? Or maybe

she was just some combination of all those identities. Maybe she was none of them.

And why did it matter, anyway? She would be
leaving Endicott in a matter of days. She could go
anywhere she wanted to go, be anything she wanted
to be. Just what she wanted—another chance to
reinvent herself again. Maybe this time, it would
stick.

Then she realized she didn't want to reinvent
herself again. She'd started kind of liking herself
this week. She'd liked how right it felt being back
in Endicott. And she liked how she'd felt whenever
she was with Max. She felt like she belonged here.
This week was the first time in a long time she'd
been comfortable, truly comfortable, anywhere.
She'd felt happy this week. Relaxed. Pleasant.
Mostly because of Max, but not entirely. Endicott
had been her home longer than anywhere else. It
was the place that formed her. It was the only place
that had ever actually felt like home. Even with the
not exactly ideal family life she'd grown up with,
this town was still the only place where she'd been
happy. She didn't want to leave now.

But how could she stay? Even if she wasn't broke,
she couldn't live where she would see Max on a
regular basis, knowing how much he hated her and
how much she lo— How much she cared for him.

"Well, I won't keep you, dear," Mrs. Barclay said as she set her empty mug on the table. "I just wanted to say hello and catch up a bit." She stood, then tucked her chair back under the table. "And to remind you that I'll see you tonight at the gala." She smiled. "You have a wonderful day, Marcy." And then, for reasons Marcy couldn't begin to understand, she added, "And bring that nice Max Travers with you."

Mrs. Barclay laughed lightly and shook a finger when she saw Marcy start to deny their involvement. "Oh, no, you don't," she said without letting Marcy speak. "I saw you two together at Mr. Aizawa's talk on Tuesday night, and you both looked just as adorable together then as you always did whenever I saw the two of you at the library when you were in school. You two always just seemed so perfect together."

And then, with a wave, she was turning and making her way out of the room, leaving Marcy dumbfounded. There was that word again—*perfect*. And it made no more sense coming from Mrs. Barclay than it had when Max said it last night.

Max couldn't remember the last time he'd been so nervous. He never got nervous. About anything. Even things most normal people got nervous

about—public speaking, flying, dentist appoint-
ments, the menu at the Cheesecake Factory—
didn't bother him at all. Yet, tonight, standing in
a gorgeous house with his two best friends since
childhood, staring out at a crowd of perfectly nice
people, many of whom he called friends and acquaintances, Max felt like he was going to throw
up. Because the moment he entered Mrs. Barclay's ballroom, his gaze had immediately lit on
one member of that crowd in particular—Marcy
Hanlon, who was standing less than half a room
away with her old friends Amanda and Claire,
chatting with much animation, as if no time at all
had passed between the three friends.

And she was wearing a blue dress again, this
one slim and figure-hugging and made of some
silky fabric that left her shoulders bare. She was
as beautiful as she had been the last time he'd seen
her in this room, fifteen years ago. Back then,
she'd had her long hair twisted up on top of her
head, and she'd been wearing makeup. He'd never
seen her in makeup before that night. Or so dressed
up. He hadn't been able to take his eyes off her.
She'd just been so perf—

No. Not perfect. Beautiful, yes. Dazzling, yes.
Kind, smart, funny, yes. But not perfect. He had
to stop thinking of her that way.

"Dude, is that Bucky Klopnik?" Chance asked beside him, pulling him out of his thoughts. "I was wondering if he'd make it."

Chance had brought as his dates for the party tonight his niece and nephew, but they were happily ensconced in the children's room with the other kids of guests, all of them contributing to a papier-mâché solar system that would be revealed at the end of the night. Felix had brought an actual date, his elusive—and very interesting—neighbor, Rory Vincent, who he was suddenly introducing as Rory Venturi for some reason he said he'd explain later, but, whatever. Max had no idea how the two of them had gone from cool acquaintances to clingy lovebirds within a matter of days, but...

Oh, wait. Maybe he did know that. He was just trying not to dwell on it at the moment. Especially not with Marcy in the room. Not even noticing him.

Anyway.

"Holy crow, Bucky came all the way from Australia for this?" Max asked, trying to at least pretend he was keeping track.

"Yeah, didn't you hear what he wished for?" Felix asked.

"Something about revenge, I think?" Max said.

"Oh, yeah," Chance assured him. "Remember,

back when we were in middle school, and Gordy Wooldridge swindled Bucky's mom out of her late husband's life insurance and disappeared, to never be seen again?"

Max nodded. "That guy was such a prick."

"Yah, well, Bucky wished Gordy would come back to town this year, turn himself in to Judge Cecil, repay his mom every penny he stole from her, plus interest, *and* that he'd do it all wearing nothing but a neon green G-string and a sign on his back that said, 'Kick me, I'm scum,' *and* that all he would have left to his name would be a Hello Kitty thermos full of rancid apple juice and a bad case of the clap."

"Wow, that's…specific," Max said.

"Yeah, Bucky was pretty steamed," Felix replied. "And you know how creative those drama kids could be."

This was true. "So did he get his wish?" Max asked.

"Yep," Felix told them. "Right down to G-string and the Hello Kitty thermos. I heard it from Deb at the diner, who told me that Veronica at the vintage shop overheard Mr. Kapileo at King Klothing telling Mr. Tucker from the train shop all about it."

"Well, then, it must be true," Chance concluded.

"Because the Endicott telegraph gossip line is never, ever wrong."

And there it was, Max thought. Another wish coming true for someone. He reminded himself that his had come true, too. He just hadn't worded it well enough. He couldn't fault others for winning their fifteen-year-old hearts' desires. He should have been as specific with his wish as Bucky had been with his. Then maybe Marcy would have seen him as, say, the kid who wouldn't even think of stealing anything from her family. Or the guy who would be there for her whenever she needed him. Or the person she couldn't live without. Or the man who would love her forever.

Yeah, that last one. That would have been nice. Because, the thing was, Max was going to love Marcy forever. He'd realized that at some point as he watched her walk down his long, long drive the night before, never looking back at him once. And as he'd been lying in bed last night, replaying every word of their exchange, he'd realized that, on some level, she'd kind of been right about him. Not so much that he was a bigot as that he was unfair. Unfair for forcing her into some idealized version of herself she could never be. Unfair for expecting her to conform herself to his definition of what she should be, not her own. All because that was what *he* wanted her to be.

Hell, hadn't he gone off on her for doing the exact same thing to him the night before that? Trying to make him into something he wasn't to make herself feel better? The difference was that she had acknowledged her mistake and apologized for it. The difference was that she had extended an olive branch and tried to work things out. The difference was that she was a big enough person to admit her mistakes—because she wasn't perfect—and learn from them and try to do better. While Max…

Well. Max wasn't perfect, either. He was willing to learn from his mistakes and try to do better, too. He just hoped he wasn't too late. Because he did love Marcy. No matter who she was. No, she wasn't perfect. But she was perfect for him. He just hoped he hadn't messed things up so badly between them that he couldn't make amends.

"Hey, I gotta go talk to somebody," he told his friends.

As one, Chance and Felix looked at Marcy, and Rory's gaze trailed theirs. Obviously, they'd seen her, too. He'd told them about what happened. About how Bob had granted his wish, the same way the comet had granted theirs, just not quite with the same happy outcome. They looked back at Max now.

"Don't screw it up, man," Chance told him. "Say everything you need to say."

Wise words, Max thought, coming from a man who'd just seen a woman he cared a lot about go back to a life that didn't include him. The twins' temporary guardian Max had met at Chance's earlier in the week had gone back to Boston, leaving Chance more than a little heartbroken. Though, after what Max had seen between the two of them even in the short span of one evening, it made him think their story wasn't quite finished yet. Even so, maybe right now, Chance was thinking he should have said more to her, too.

"Yeah, *mijo*," Felix added. He looped an arm around Rory's waist, pulling her close with much affection. "It's amazing, the power words can have."

Rory leaned into Felix, and she smiled. "Just be yourself," she told him. "That's pretty powerful, too. And good luck," she added softly.

Max inhaled a deep, fortifying breath, then made his way into the crowd. By the time he reached Marcy, Claire had drifted off to rejoin her partner, and Amanda was heading to the bar. Marcy turned around, then halted when she saw Max standing there. For a moment, she looked at him the way she had earlier in the week, before everything went to hell, taking in his khakis and gray jacket and the button-down shirt striped with both colors. He'd actually made his sister, Lilah, come over that afternoon to dress him, because he'd wanted to make a good impression tonight. And in that first moment Marcy looked at him, he could tell he had. Then her expression soured a bit, and the temperature around them seemed to drop.

"Hello, Max," she said frostily.

"Hey, Marcy," he replied warmly.

Between the two of them, the temperature seemed to adjust a bit. At least she stopped frowning at him.

"Um, could we talk?" he asked her.

Her eyebrows shot up. "The way I wanted to talk last night, but then you told me we don't have anything to talk about? That way?"

He knew he had the rebuke coming. And he knew he deserved it. It didn't make it any easier to handle.

"Yeah, like that," he told her. "Only, this time, I will have something to say."

She met his gaze levelly. "Unless it's 'I'm sorry, Marcy, I was wrong,' then I don't think there's any point in—"

"I'm sorry, Marcy, I was wrong," he interjected.

She still had her mouth open at his admission, but then closed it. She looked at him silently for another couple of uncomfortable seconds, then said, "Oh. Well, then. I guess we could talk."

"Thanks."

The crowd around them seemed to have doubled in size during just that short exchange, so Max gestured toward a set of open doors he knew led out to a terrace and, beyond that, a garden. Marcy fell into step beside him and, taking a chance, he reached for her free hand and wove her fingers with his. At first, she kept hers stiff and straight. But after a couple of seconds, she relaxed them, settling her hand comfortably into his. Then they were heading outside, into the cool September night.

A little too cool maybe, he realized when the breeze wafted over them. Not only could he feel the chill, but he also saw Marcy's skin pebble with gooseflesh. Without a word, he took off his jacket and draped it over her shoulders, and, without a word, she let him. Then, after a moment, she pulled it closed around herself. And in that moment, Max almost felt like it was him who was embracing her.

"Thanks," she said.

"You're welcome," he told her.

As if in tacit agreement, they tangled their fingers together again and continued to walk. Past the handful of people mingling on the terrace, past the few more mingling on the path, until they were nearly at the edge of the garden. Max led her to a bench near a gathering of lobelias—he knew they would be there, because he planted and took care of Mrs. Barclay's garden, too—and they both sat down. When Marcy saw the flowers there, she smiled. Then she seemed to remember that she was still mad at him—fair enough—and the smile vanished. But its brief appearance gave Max a ray of hope to cling to, and for the first time in days, he felt like maybe, just maybe, his wish really would come true the way he'd hoped it would fifteen years ago.

"You were right last night," he said without preamble. "Not so much that I'm a bigot," he clarified. "But I am biased. And I am unfair. Or, at least, I was. I always expected you to behave in a way that's stereotypical and archaic.

"The alabaster goddess of all that's good who's just not capable of or allowed to make mistakes," he added, injecting a woo-woo quality into his voice. Then he sighed. "Put it down to reading too many bad fantasy novels as a kid. Put it down to just being a kid. A dumb kid, at that, one who never quite outgrew the idea that the girl he liked at fifteen was perfect. No one is perfect," he conceded. "Not you. Not me. When I was telling you to take a better look at yourself, I should have told myself that, too. I'm sorry I was so narrow-minded. And biased. And unfair."

She studied him closely for a moment, as if she was digesting everything he'd said and aligning it with her own words and thoughts and feelings of a couple of nights ago. Then, softly, she said, "I'm sorry I was all those things, too. I didn't mean to be. I guess, like you said, some things we just take longer to outgrow than others."

"But you know what?" Max said. "The beauty of making mistakes is that we can learn from them. And we can do better next time." He hoped he didn't sound like a cringey fifteen-year-old when he added, "If, you know, there is a next time."

Nope, he totally sounded like a cringey fifteen-year-old. But Marcy didn't seem to mind. She laughed lightly. "I'd like for there to be a next time. I'd like for there to be a lot of next times. I think you and I have a lot to learn about each other. And I'd like very much to learn everything I can about you, Max."

Only when she said that did Max realize how very much he'd been fearing she would tell him to shove off. He didn't kid himself that the two of them didn't still have a bit of work to do. But it was good work. And they'd be doing it together. And that…

Well, he hated to say it but…that was kind of perfect.

"I want to learn everything there is about you, too," he said.

For another moment, they only looked at each other in silence, almost as if they were seeing each other for the first time. Then, ever so slowly, Marcy scooted a little closer to Max. So Max moved himself a little closer to her. She scooched a few more inches toward him. So he pushed himself the last couple of inches toward her, until their bodies were touching.

"Hey, look at that," he said. "We met right in the middle."

Marcy smiled. Max smiled. Then, as one, they dipped their heads toward each other. This time, when they kissed, it was almost as if they were two kids doing it for the first time. Tentatively, slowly, experimentally. Again and again, their lips brushed against each other, until Max felt the heat rising inside him to the point where he knew they were going to need to be alone together soon. So, reluctantly, he pulled away. Marcy, too, seemed to have been as moved as he was by the gentle gesture. She cupped his cheek in one hand and touched her forehead to his. For several moments, she said nothing. Then she sat back again and gazed at him, in a way that made him feel as if she was seeing him for the first time.

Finally, he asked, "What are you thinking about?"

She expelled a soft sound that was a mixture of marvel, contentment and relief. "I'm just thinking about what a great job Bob did making my wish come true. I didn't think it was going to happen for me. But it did, just now."

Max realized his wish had come true, too, finally. At least in the way he had wanted it to fifteen years ago. "What did you wish for?" he asked Marcy.

She hesitated a moment, but finally told him, "I wished Bob would give me someone who could make everything okay. The last time he came around, I felt like everything in my life was terrible, the way a lot of fifteen-year-old girls do. Just the usual melodramatic ups and downs of adolescence that seemed so much more important than they really were. So I wished for Bob to give me someone who could make everything okay.

"Then, this year, when everything in my life really was falling apart, I knew I needed that wish to come true more than ever. So I came back to Endicott to see if Bob would grant my wish. And he did.

Because you, Max, you make everything okay. Better than okay. You make everything…" She smiled. "Perfect," she said with a light laugh. "At least, you make it perfect for me. I think maybe I kind of… love you."

The warmth that had been rising in Max went incandescent at that admission. His wish to Bob really had come true. Marcy saw him as someone who could make everything okay. She saw him as someone who was perfect for her. The same way she was perfect for him. She saw him as someone she loved.

"I love you, too," he said, hoping the words didn't come out in the rush it felt like. Then he kissed her again. And then he looked up at the sky. "Thanks, Bob," he said.

She looked up, too. "Yeah, nicely done." Then she looked at Max. "Wait, you never told me what you wished for."

He'd been fearing she would ask that. "Yeah, it's kind of complicated," he told her. "I'll explain it all later, if you're not doing anything after the gala."

"I'm not doing anything after the gala," she said immediately, her words rushed, too. Then she added, "At least tell me if your wish came true."

He nodded. "Better than I ever could have hoped."

"I look forward to hearing all about it," she said. "After the gala. Which should be ending soon."

"Maybe we could go back to my place for a little while," he suggested.

"A little while," she echoed with another smile. "Yeah, that'd be nice."

He had a moment of panic at her words when he remembered how she had hinted at the possibility that she'd be leaving town soon. Surely, she wasn't still planning to do that. Was she?

"I mean, you can stay for longer than a little while," he quickly amended. "It's not like I have any plans to go anywhere any time soon."

His panic must have been showing in his expression, because she lifted her hand to his cheek again, brushed a quick kiss over his lips and told him, "I'm not going anywhere, either. I'm staying here in Endicott. Amanda generously offered me the use of her spare room for a week or two, until I can find a place of my own. And Mrs. Jeffs at Jeffs Jewelers made me a nice offer on my wedding band, which I so don't need anymore." She smiled. "I'm not sure exactly what I'll do yet, but Hanlon House had a notice up that they're hiring. Maybe I can get something there until I start writing again." She looked troubled for a moment. "*If* I ever start writing again," she added.

The comment confused him. "Why wouldn't you start writing again?" he asked.

But she just shook her head. "That's complicated, too. I'll tell you all about it at your place later. Anyway, I'm pretty sure a Hanlon could get a job at Hanlon House in some capacity."

The wind picked up again, and Marcy pulled his jacket closer. When Max suggested they go back inside, she readily agreed. They found Chance and Felix and Rory sitting at a table on the other side of the ballroom and joined them, Max introducing the two women for the first time and Felix and Chance echoing their delight at seeing Marcy again. Not long after that, the children who had been working on their solar system, including Chance's niece and nephew, Quinn and Finn, entered the ballroom with their creation. They, in turn, found their way to their uncle and scrambled onto his lap, chattering with much excitement about all the new friends they'd made.

Max couldn't help thinking how all three men's lives had changed so much in less than a week's time. But none of them seemed to mind the changes much. Or, you know, at all. Bob had been generous this year. He wondered where they'd all be the next time the comet came around.

He was about to speak the thought aloud, but he

was interrupted by overhearing a trio of voices at the table beside them sharing what was the most often uttered question at the party tonight: *What did you wish for?* When he turned in his seat, he saw three girls he guessed to be around fifteen years old talking among themselves the way teen-age girls tended to do at big parties—loudly.

"Shut up!" said one. "You did not wish you would be Seamus O'Connor's, uh… What did you say you wished you would be for Seamus O'Connor again?"

The girl sitting next to her sighed deeply. "His *grá fíor*," she said in a dreamy voice. "I wished I would be his *grá fíor*. It's Celtic, or maybe Gaelic— I can't remember—for 'true love.'"

"Are you sure that's what it means?" the third girl asked.

"Of course, I'm sure. I googled it."

"Do you think Comet Bob speaks Celtic or Gaelic?" the third girl asked. "And are you sure you pronounced it correctly? 'Cause, not gonna lie, it kinda sounded like you wished you would be Seamus's great fear."

Max bit back a chuckle. To her credit, the second girl seemed a little concerned. Before she could say anything, though, the first girl looked at the third and asked, "What did you wish for?"

The third girl sat up proudly in her chair. "I wished I would be the greatest pastry chef in the world. Easy-peasy."

"Easy-peasy," the first girl echoed dubiously. "Heard that before. From you, as a matter of fact. Right before that croquembouche blew up in your face in food science class. Now, I ask you. How do you blow up a croquembouche? How does that even happen?"

"That was then," the third girl answered without concern. "This is the future. I'll be a much better baker by then. What did you wish for?"

The first girl looked smug. "*I* wished for something really good. I wished for something that we'll *all* benefit from."

"Uh-huh," said girl number two, clearly unimpressed. "What was it?"

Girl number one looked first at one friend, then the other. "I wished something *fabulous* would happen in this town for once."

Max nearly lost it at that. He looked at Marcy and, when he realized she had overheard the conversation, too, he smiled.

She smiled back. "Don't you dare say it to them," she cautioned him.

He feigned innocence. "Don't say what?"

"Do not tell them that they better be careful what they wish for, because they might get it."

"Now, why would I do something like that?"

"Max…" she said, her warning unmistakable.

He opened his mouth theatrically, as if he was going to shout that very warning to the rooftops. Then he closed it again. "Nah. Let them learn that for themselves in fifteen years. Like we did."

"And then they can thank their lucky stars. Like we did."

She smiled abruptly, in a way he'd never quite seen her smile this week. As if she'd suddenly become delighted by something she hadn't expected.

"What?" he asked her. "What are you thinking?"

She didn't say anything for a moment but seemed to be deep in thought. She held up a hand, one finger extended, as if she would answer that question in just a second, as soon as she…

As soon as she pulled out her phone and started frantically typing?

"What?" Max asked again. "What are you doing?"

She held up the finger again, for just a nanosecond, then went back to furiously writing something down on her phone. He waited as long as he could for her to finish, but at the rate she was going, it would be morning before she told him anything.

"Marcy, what are you doing?" he asked again.

Still furiously typing, she told him, "I'm making some notes. Hearing those girls talk, I got a really good idea for a book. This great coming-of-age story about three girls and a wish-granting comet. Just…gimme a couple minutes to get some ideas down. It's like they're just pouring into my brain. And…don't talk to me until further notice." Without looking up, she gestured at the others sitting at the table with them. "Talk amongst yourselves."

Max chuckled. Was this what it was going to be like, living with a writer? He couldn't wait.

He looked up at the ceiling, at the whimsical painting of the solar system with Comet Bob at its center, surrounded by glittering stars. And he sent another silent thank-you to the heavens above. Life was good. For all of them. Thanks to a wish, and a comet, and a little bit of luck from the stars.

* * * * *

Don't miss the other books in the Lucky Stars miniseries:

Be Careful What You Wish For
Her Good-Luck Charm

Available now wherever Harlequin Special Edition books and ebooks are sold!

#2947 THE MAVERICK'S CHRISTMAS SECRET
Montana Mavericks: Brothers & Broncos • by Brenda Harlen
Ranch hand Sullivan Grainger came to Bronco to learn the truth about his twin's disappearance. All he's found so far is more questions—and an unexpected friendship with his late brother's sister-in-law, Sadie Chamberlin. The sweet and earnest shopkeeper offers Sullivan a glimpse of how full his life could be, if only he could release the past and embrace Sadie's Christmas spirit!

#2948 STARLIGHT AND THE CHRISTMAS DARE
Welcome to Starlight • by Michelle Major
Madison Mauer is trying to be content with her new life working in a small town bar but is still surprised when her boss-mandated community work leads to some unexpected friendships, including a teenage delinquent. The girl's older brother is another kind of surprise—and they're all in need of some second chances this Christmas!

#2949 THEIR TEXAS CHRISTMAS MATCH
Lockharts Lost & Found • by Cathy Gillen Thacker
A sudden inheritance stipulates commitment-phobes Skye McPherson and Travis Lockhart must marry and live together for a hundred and twenty days. A quick, temporary marriage is clearly the easiest solution. Until Skye discovers she's pregnant with her new husband's baby and Travis starts falling for his short-term wife. With a million reasons to leave, will love win out this Christmas?

#2950 LIGHTS, CAMERA...WEDDING?
Sutter Creek, Montana • by Laurel Greer
Fledgling florist Bea Halloran has banked her business and love life on her upcoming reality TV Christmas wedding. When her fiancé walks out, Bea's best friend, Brody Emerson, steps in as the fake groom, saving her business...and making her feel passion she barely recognizes. And Brody's smoldering glances and knee-weakening kisses might just put their platonic vows to the test...

#2951 EXPECTING HIS HOLIDAY SURPRISE
Gallant Lake Stories • by Jo McNally
Jade is focused on her new bakery and soon, raising her new baby. When Jade's one-night stand, Trent Mitchell, unexpectedly shows up, it's obvious that their chemistry is real. Until Jade's fierce independence clashes with Trent's doubts about fatherhood. Is their magic under the mistletoe strong enough to make them a forever family?

#2952 COUNTERFEIT COURTSHIP
Heart & Soul • by Synithia Williams
When a kiss at a reality TV wedding is caught on camera, there's only one way to save *his* reputation and *her* career. Now paranormal promoter Tyrone Livingston and makeup artist Kiera Fox are officially dating. But can a relationship with an agreed-upon end date turn into a real and lasting love?

**YOU CAN FIND MORE INFORMATION ON UPCOMING HARLEQUIN TITLES,
FREE EXCERPTS AND MORE AT HARLEQUIN.COM.**

HSECNM1022

"I'm going to call my friend who's a nurse in the morning. She's not working in that capacity now, but she grew up in this town. She'll help get you with a good physical therapist."

The warmth she'd seen in his eyes disappeared, and she told herself it shouldn't matter. It was better they remember who they were to each other—people who had a troubled girl in common but nothing more.

She couldn't allow it to be anything more.

"You need a Christmas tree," he said as she started to back away.

"I didn't see any decorations in your house."

He nodded. "Yeah, but Stella made me promise I would at least get a tree."

"I'll consider a tree," Madison told him. It felt like a small concession. "Although I'm not much for Christmas spirit."

"That makes two of us."

Once again, she wasn't sure how to feel about having something in common with Chase.

He cleared his throat. "I have more work to do—meetings and deadlines to reschedule. I can make it back to the bedroom."

"I'll see you tomorrow."

"I'll be here." He laughed without humor. "It's not like I can get anywhere else."

"Good night, Chase."

"Good night, Madison," he answered.

The words felt close to a caress, and she hurried to her bedroom before her knees started to melt.

Don't miss
Starlight and the Christmas Dare *by Michelle Major,*
available December 2022 wherever
Harlequin Special Edition books and ebooks are sold.

Harlequin.com

HSEEXP1022

HARLEQUIN
PLUS

Announcing a **BRAND-NEW**
multimedia subscription service
for romance fans like you!

Read, Watch and Play.

Experience the easiest way to get
the romance content you crave.

Start your **FREE 7 DAY TRIAL** at
<u>www.harlequinplus.com/freetrial</u>.

Love Harlequin romance?

DISCOVER.

Be the first to find out about promotions,
news and exclusive content!

f Facebook.com/HarlequinBooks

🐦 Twitter.com/HarlequinBooks

📷 Instagram.com/HarlequinBooks

📌 Pinterest.com/HarlequinBooks

You Tube YouTube.com/HarlequinBooks

ReaderService.com

EXPLORE.

Sign up for the Harlequin e-newsletter and
download a free book from any series at
TryHarlequin.com

CONNECT.

Join our Harlequin community to
share your thoughts and connect
with other romance readers!
Facebook.com/groups/HarlequinConnection